For Pegg...

Tales From Alberta Muskeg Country

to diversity in nature
Elaine Strom

BY ELAINE STROM

◆ FriesenPress

One Printers Way
Altona, MB R0G 0B0
Canada

www.friesenpress.com

Author Photo: credit to photographer Rochelle-Ann Thomas, CSD Media,
Calgary AB

DISCLAIMER: This collection of short stories is a work of fiction. The
characters and any of their names, as well as any events, incidents, or business
establishments as depicted and developed in this collection, are fictitious. Any
resemblance to real persons, living or dead, or to real life events, is coincidental.

ISBN
978-1-03-913790-5 (Hardcover)
978-1-03-913789-9 (Paperback)
978-1-03-913791-2 (eBook)

1. BISAC code 001

Distributed to the trade by The Ingram Book Company

Acknowledgements

I would like to express my enormous gratitude to my writing mentor, Sally Hatcher, who is the facilitator of the writing group of which I am a member. Sally's academic credentialing—a Master's Degree in English—as well as, her adherence to professionalism immediately secured my confidence with regard to her competence and reliability.

Her inviting and respectful writing environment, relaxed structure, and encouraging belief in and commitment to hearing each writer's *voice* have allowed me to realize my potential capacity for attempting varied writing techniques. I am indebted to her strong assessment skills, constructive critiquing, and a consistent resoluteness.

I have also greatly appreciated endorsements from my son, members of my writing group, and random friends. Their inquiries of interest have been a source of encouragement and have served to bolster my confidence. Any disclosures that they, too, harbour aspirations to write, have elicited an immediate area of interest in common.

Preface

The fictional stories of this collection are based on my experiences while having lived, worked, and travelled in a particular area of northern Alberta muskeg country. They take place on the fringe of frontier living in isolation. My reflections on these areas and environments, as well as, the fictional characters in these stories, exude with awe and inspiration, respect and reverence, the testing of personal limits, and sometimes, the harshness of the final moments prior to imminent death.

My time in northern Alberta was a unique experience for me, an exposure to new cultures and ways of life. I valued that experience and did not want to forget, as tends to happen over time.

Self-expression through writing has always seemed to come naturally to me. Therefore, as recollections from my time in the north came to mind, I would jot them down. However, life was always busy, and I never had the time to develop them.

The years have passed, and the time seems right to finally attend to those recollections that, still today, hold a persisting place in my mind. I am retired now, and currently coping with the COVID-19 pandemic, related social distancing, and self-isolation. In other words, I have time.

I hope that my stories leave you with a sense of having been there with me. I hope that I impart my connection with nature. I hope that you feel the emotions of loneliness, frustration, fear, and compassion that I experienced. And, I hope that you experience some of what I learned.

ARCTIC COLD

Cutting cold pierces my lungs as I attempt to breathe. I can only manage short little breaths, or I begin to cough. The cold cuts through my hands like a knife. As I exhale, my face is constantly wet from the condensation on my wrap-around scarf, and it chafes at my chin.

Jimmy McPherson is my name, but my friends have always called me Red. I suppose it was because of my carrot-red hair from the day I was born, and my sun-burnt nose and ears every summer. It seems the freckles could not protect all of me.

I arrived to the town of High Prairie, Alberta only a month ago-straight out of college-to start work as a forestry technician in the provincial sub-office here. My usual shift starts at five a.m. at which time I diligently venture out to my assigned fleet truck in the company parking lot in order to start and let the engine warm.

The intense cold now probes deep into my brow. I instinctively retreat downward into the insulating warmth of my hooded coyote fur parka, which makes me think of my mom and dad back home in Saskatchewan. My dad traps coyotes when the culling seasons are open and usually sells the pelts. But on occasion, he keeps them for his personal use. And, in turn, my mom, a skilled seamstress and custom designer, creates all kinds of fur fashions from them, and in fact, made this fur parka for me. If she only knew how grateful I am right now, I think to myself.

I secure my hood in place with a long Saskatchewan Roughriders scarf that some friends gave me as a send-off gift the night before I left for Alberta; I love it. Ahh, that feels much warmer I tell myself. I also pause to tightly tuck my ski pants into my knee-high snow boots—anything to keep that cold air out. But my toes are toasty warm in thick wool socks that my mom had knit with yarn she cards and spins after the late spring shearing on the farm.

Lastly, I put on my wide-cuffed deerskin mitts and have lined those with a wool pair my mom had knit for me before I left. I am very aware that I have already acquired quite the identity around town, entirely attributable to my parka, scarf, and mitts. "There goes that new guy from Saskatchewan," I hear them say.

I proudly purchased my beautifully handcrafted mitts from a travelling salesman when I first arrived in High Prairie. I liked the smoky smell of the soft, caramel-brown, tanned hide; the colourful and swirling red, blue, and white flower Indigenous bead work design on the front of the mitts; and most of all, the thick soft tufts of light-brown moose hair around the wrists and cuffs.

However, I soon realized these mitts did not bode well with the discerning eyes of the Woodland Cree Indigenous people around me. A chance encounter with a wise and kind Indigenous female elder in the community explained to me one day, that given the design and colours of the bead work, along with the moose hair tufting, I was wearing mitts that had been crafted by the Indigenous people of northern Manitoba, and not Alberta. Nevertheless, I liked my mitts and I determined to wear them-with both a respect for whomever had crafted them, as well as a readily self-professed newcomer naivety about the cultures around me.

I feel like such a stranger here, to everyone and everything around me, and I feel so alone. I wish my wife and kids were here with me but, I'm going through a divorce.

I married a girl from the Maritimes-Nova Scotia, to be exact. Her name is Rhona and we had both just graduated from high school and had been working for the summer in Prince Albert National Park in northern Saskatchewan when we met. She had been a waitress in the resort town of Waskesiu Lake, and I had been a groundskeeper at the Beaver Glen campground.

In retrospect, it's clear to me why we had been attracted to each other. On our very first encounter, Rhona had told me how much she was missing her family and home back east and how lonely she felt. Nevertheless, I found her to be delightfully sociable, and soon discovered, too, that she played a mean fiddle across a campfire. As for me, having grown up on the farm and being right out of high school, I had not experienced life out on my own yet. I did find, however, that I was always securely in my comfort zone as long as I could be in the fresh outdoors.

Rhona and I would meet up at each day's end, roasting whatever food we had over the fire, laughing about the difficulties of our day, chatting about our home life and families, and listening to the eerie, haunting, and mournful summer breeding call of the loons across the moonlit lake.

Within the next five years, we married and had two children. My girl was five and my boy was three years old when we split. I realized too late that my relationship with Rhona should have stayed a summer fling. Sadly, we came to know that we were not well-suited for one another. True, I had paternal roots back in Nova Scotia, but we came from very different lifestyle backgrounds. I had grown up in farming and ranching country in southern Saskatchewan, and she had come from generational livelihoods of fishing. I had come right off the farm, and she was constantly missing her family, friends, and Maritime culture.

The fact that we came from different worlds could, perhaps, have worked to our advantage if we had been financially independent, and for example, could have had the means to pursue travel and adventure as a family. But I was not prepared for the responsibility of marriage and family and had no post-secondary training toward any career path. Neither of us had been in a good place to be committing to a permanent relationship so soon in our lives.

After we married, we moved in with my parents and helped out on the farm. But, with no money of our own, and my parents unable to afford to keep us, our future soon looked bleak.

It wasn't long before the fighting started. Rhona had become very depressed as her loneliness worsened. I felt that we were a burden on my parents; I felt like a failure, and became increasingly moody and short-tempered. As an escape, I had started drinking and hanging out with the boys.

One morning, after the children had gone out to play, my wife nervously, but with a firm resolve in her voice, announced to me and my parents "I have plane tickets to Halifax for both me and the kids. We'll be leaving today." Her chin quivered and her head momentarily fell as she disclosed "You know I don't have that kind of money; I asked my family, some time ago, for help to get back to Nova Scotia." The silence had been awkwardly deafening.

Rhona had looked tired and thin. With tears in her eyes, she had looked at me in earnest as she told me "Jimmy, it would be better for all of us if you would say goodbye to the children here." She then looked toward my parents and, with hesitation, flatly stated "I could use a ride to the Saskatoon airport. Our things are already packed. There is someone I can call if I am asking too much." Rhona was taking the children and leaving me. I had felt this moment might be coming for some time, yet still, I found myself speechless, motionless, and numb in disbelief.

My parents had glanced at one another in silence, their faces ashen and grim. It seemed to me that they had known this would inevitably happen. My father was the first to respond. His mouth sounded dusty dry and there was a tightness in his throat as he informed us, "I know that one of the neighbours is planning a trip to Saskatoon today, leaving around noon. He will be driving his half-ton truck and probably travelling alone. I feel certain he'd be happy to help out. I'll give him a call Rhona." The neighbour arrived shortly before noon, and quickly loaded Rhona's two large suitcases into the back of his truck.

The children had not been able to comprehend what was happening. They were worried and sad, and kept asking, "Why are you crying Daddy?" The words just did not come to me. I merely held their little hands—feeling the innocent softness.

My parents had tried to console the children and, with tears streaming down their faces, had held them close as they whispered "Grandma and Grandpa love you so very very much. We will try and come to visit you real soon." My wife and I had not been able to touch, nor even speak to each other. The emotional pain of parting, for both of us, had been more than we could bear in the moment.

The neighbour had quietly pulled out of the yard, slowly rolled down the lane way, and finally turned onto the municipal road that heads toward the highway. It tore my parents' hearts out to watch their grandchildren leaving. I watched for as long as I could, until the truck's trail of dust disappeared into the distance.

A squeezing, constricting pain clutched at my throat and the penetrating ache from my clenched jaw was unbearable. I left the house and walked toward a grove of poplar trees where I slumped to the ground, nestling into the cool, cushioning seclusion of the tall, waving broom grasses. I began to sob—an uncontrollable, rasping sob—until my guts could no longer endure the reefing.

I lingered in the grass for several hours, listening to the rustle of the leaves and welcoming the obscurity around me. Finally, with clarity of vision and a determined resolve, I got up and calmly walked back to the house.

Supper had been prepared and waiting for some time. As we began to eat, my parents and I sat around the kitchen table in painful, staring silence. "I'm going to apply to start college in Saskatoon in the fall," I said, my voice breaking as I avoided looking into their eyes. "I'm hoping to get accepted into the Forestry Technician diploma program. It's just a year." I quickly added. "I will be applying for a government student loan." My parents simultaneously rose up from the table, wrapped their arms around me, and held me for what seemed a very long time.

"We'll always be there for you son," my dad said.

"And we will help you any way we can," my mom added, her voice breaking just as mine had.

The summer had gone quickly as there was always work to do on the farm, in addition to the college entrance requirements I had to take care of. Upon submitting my application, I had received mail verification almost immediately that I was admitted into the program. I was ecstatic! I felt like such a burden had been lifted. I now had new purpose and direction in my life.

Because I was going to be operating on a student loan, I committed to as little spending as possible. I had taken the Greyhound bus to Saskatoon to begin college, and I was on foot to get around after that as I couldn't afford the added costs of operating and maintaining a vehicle. I stayed in residence and shared a room with a young guy just out of high school and who was from a Ukrainian community northeast of Saskatoon. He came from a farming background, as well, so we were never at a loss for something to talk about.

My roommate went home for all the holidays and his parents frequently came in to the city, which allowed me much appreciated space and privacy. But, what I wholeheartedly appreciated, even more, was the home baking and cooking my roommate would bring back with him after each and every visit with his parents: Ukrainian breads and sweets, perogies with all kinds of different fillings, borscht, and cabbage rolls. And the more I told my roommate to be sure and tell his mom how much I had enjoyed him sharing them, the more she sent next time.

I found it hard to be confined to classrooms and my residential quarters after being used to outdoor wide open spaces on the farm. But, I liked my courses and spent all my free time studying; it kept me busy and my mind occupied, no time to dwell on my problems.

I was well-liked by my classmates and instructors, and probably due to my older age more than anything, was often designated as a team leader on projects. However, I did decline invites out to socialize as I just could not afford to participate nor share in any expenses. And, although everyone knew I had a family and was going through a divorce, I was not willing to disclose any specifics, not yet. It hurt too much and I was still sorting things out in my own mind.

I feel a lot of guilt about the way I had chosen to cope with my marriage and financial situation and about the way I had behaved toward Rhona, my kids, and my parents; I constantly miss them all. My parents have committed to sending Rhona whatever financial support they can spare each month for the grandchildren, at least until she and I become more stable in terms of our employment. I feel ashamed that it's my parents that have had to do that; it should be my responsibility. Rhona and the kids moved in with her parents. She got a couple of part-time jobs right away, and with the money my parents have been sending, she has been able to get by. My parents couldn't afford, of course, to be driving back and forth to the city to visit with me, too, but my mom would send a letter from time to time with news about what was happening on the farm or in the community back home.

The divorce process is now amicable enough but "God, how I miss my kids!" I find myself telling people over, and over, and over again. So much has happened in their lives since they left. My girl is now six years old and in Grade 1, and my boy, now four, is in play school. I should have been a part of all that. My telephone call on their birthdays is not enough. I feel like I am losing touch with them. For the holidays, my little girl can now print a rudimentary note and, along with my boy, always draws a picture for me. Rhona, it seems, makes sure it all gets into the mail. Likewise, I communicate back to the kids and they have told me they really liked the college pamphlets I had sent with pictures of where I was staying and what I was doing.

A year later, I graduated at the top of my class. My parents were so proud and attended my graduation ceremony, taking lots of pictures of the conferring of my diploma. I had done it!

I had sent out several applications for employment and was delighted to have received an impressive number of job interviews. Employment would mean I now had a chance to secure a future for myself. And I was beyond ready for both the experience and the adventure. I realized it was time to grow up and be accountable; in other words, it was time to be a man. With an education and a secure job, I knew I would be able to offer financial support for my kids, have them be a part of my life again if I could afford to visit them, or maybe, as they got older, pay for them to visit me. I wanted to do well by them, and also, by my parents.

I accepted the Peace River Country job offer that was out of a provincial sub-office in the town of High Prairie. I loved the idea of working outdoors, and needless to say, was desperately attracted to the bonus offer of isolation pay as well. Based on what I had learned at college and from the job description that I had been hired for, I was expecting to be mostly protecting and preserving forest and natural resources, presumably, such things as planting, erosion control, monitoring natural water quality, protecting wildlife habitats, and so on.

High Prairie and area had seemed like a natural fit in relation to my forest technician diploma. With boreal forest extending all the way from the Lesser Slave Lake region north to the rocks and bedrock of the Pre-Cambrian Shield, an abundance of freshwater lakes, and a bustling oil and gas industry in the Red Earth Creek area, it seemed to me, there would be an obvious need for the conservation of these resources, as well as, the preservation of the environment around them. I could envision, too, that once I had a sufficient work experience, had a clearer idea of what my areas of interest and expertise were, and was better informed as to how to network in the field, there could be all kinds of opportunity for me to pursue my career goals in this geographical area, and better yet, if I had a degree in forestry. It naturally followed that if I were appropriately credentialed, I could probably work toward seeking out a promotion in future, that is, a management position for myself.

I anticipated a diversity of options that I would be able to pursue. I could potentially become immersed in the logging industries in their provision of timber and fuel wood. Or perhaps, I would prefer to become more involved in the maintenance of natural water quality, or the monitoring and maintenance of watershed areas, or in erosion control. I may want to focus more on the protection of wild life habitat, and actually, think I would really like that. Or perhaps, I would find myself more vested in the protection of the landscape and community, along with recreation development. High Prairie seemed, to me, to be a gateway hub to it all.

My thoughts shift again as I become even more acutely aware of my feelings of loneliness in this frigid, long, dark, night-into-day. Only the hard, squeaking crunch of my feet on the packed snow accompanies me. As my gaze inadvertently drifts upward, I am distracted by the heavenly winter wonder of stars above me. They are so clearly visible in this land of crisp coldness, their defining brightness unpolluted by the lights of dense urban development.

I particularly notice the Milky Way galaxy, a density of sparkling whiteness, cascading across the infinite blackness of the night sky as if it were a long bridal veil—so breathtakingly beautiful! And prominent in the north sky this early hour of the morning, I see the Big Dipper, seemingly positioned as if to catch whatever might spill from the Little Dipper hanging just above it. My eyes follow along the handle of the Little Dipper, and there, at the very tip, as if to hold the Little Dipper in place, is the North Star, the brilliantly shining yellow-white star nearest the North Pole.

I search, low in the southwestern sky, for the constellation Orion, expecting it will be there this time of year. Sure enough, I fondly recognize the three linear stars known to make up his belt, along with the bright nebular sword that hangs below. As a boy growing up in the wide-open spaces of southern Saskatchewan where the constellations are clearly visible all year 'round, and where most farmers and ranchers are avid wild meat hunters, I had been introduced to Orion early for he was known to them as the Mighty Hunter. His dogs accompany him; that is, the bright stars to his left, the *Canis Major* or "greater dog" named Syrius and above him, the *Canis Minor* or "lesser dog" named Procyon. Many a night I had drifted off to sleep, fantasizing about one hunting adventure after another while cavorting with the dogs along the way.

I recall, too, how I had always tagged along with my dad to do the chores, or would just sit with him on the farmhouse step on warm summer evenings. He was a quiet and modest man, but I learned so much from him. He would quietly talk to me as he made random observations which, in turn, captured my attention and satisfied my curiosity.

I can remember how my dad had often pointed out the constellations, telling me the Latin names and their meanings as he had learned them at school. I quickly caught on; once I knew what a name meant, I was able to connect it with what I was looking at in the sky. It had all made perfect sense in helping me to remember the constellation names.

For example, I remember connecting the Latin name *Via Lactea* with lactating milk cows and the image of the whiteness of milk, hence, the Milky Way. I think, too, how in the summertime, at the door of our farmhouse, we had kept a washstand with a water pail and drinking dipper on it to prevent the hired men from tracking through in their dirty clothes every time they wanted a drink. I related the familiarity of that dipper with remembering the names of the similar-patterned Big and Little Dippers in the sky. I also became accustomed to my dad making reference to the North Star as a point of orientation when checking directions in the black of night.

As I think back to these special times with my dad, my missing my kids becomes unbearable. I had begun to share this tradition of stargazing with them as well. My girl would take my hand as we did outdoor chores at night, accompanied by my boy, too, if he was still awake. She would hop along and eagerly plead "Daddy, tell us about the puppies in the sky again-please Daddy, please." And they would argue as to who found the North Star first. And my boy would frequently interject with the name of a part of a constellation he thought he had just seen, or perhaps, he had merely been trying to impress us, wanting us know that he had remembered any name at all. I wonder, do they still remember? Can they see them where they live now? I must ask them.

"Enough already!" I verbally reprimand myself as I finally reach my truck. "Just how long have I been thinking about all this stuff anyway? Time to get back to reality and get some work done." I breathe a sigh of relief and mutter out loud, "Well, wha' do ya' know, the extension cord is still plugged into the charging post and the receptacle end is still attached to the plug from the block heater. The motor should be warm and should start easily." "Damn those kids," I curse "when they run through this lot, yanking out the plugs and cords." But today, I optimistically determine, it looks like I'm in luck and it's going to be a good day.

Making sure all accessories are turned off, I next turn the key in the ignition. I hear a low groan; I pause, then turn the key again.

"Aha!" I declare. The motor is turning is over—a quickening, tight, high-pitched, squealing whine. "Pump the gas pedal but don't flood the damn thing!" I curse out loud. I stop, then turn the key again. "Yesss," I hiss, followed by an exuberant shout. "The spark plugs are firing, the motor's running, it's idling—shaking and vibrating, idling rough, but it's running!"

My shoulders are hunched and my knees squeezed tight together as I shiver and shake and let the motor warm up. I huddle against the first cold blast of air from the heat vents. Impatient to look at the outside world around me, I remove my right mitt in order to peel some white frost curlicues from the interior side window with my nails, then quickly put my mitt back on. I never thought I would be so grateful for a pair of my mother's rough, raw, home-knit wool mitts! I feel her love and caring in their warmth and it helps me to not feel quite so alone in this bitter black cold. I hear myself utter a spontaneous "Love ya', Mom."

My survival bag is within easy reach and I need to check that too. Before I set out on every road trip, I make it a habit to take inventory of my personal survival gear and equipment. I learned growing up in the harsh winters of Saskatchewan, and now in Alberta, to never venture out without having done that, as my life may depend on it.

Already, too many times to count, I have been in a vehicle that has spun out and ditched into snow too deep to get a door open, or have become hung up on packed snow that has drifted across the road. My dad's words ring in my head, "Always-stay with your vehicle." I have also had occasion to run the engine until I've run out of gas, trying to keep the heater going. But once the gas gauge was on EMPTY, I am only here to tell the story because of extra clothes and blankets that I had on board. Or, there have been times when I couldn't run the engine because I was so buried in snow that the exhaust pipe had become obstructed, and fumes would merely have fed back into the vehicle cabin, resulting in carbon monoxide poisoning. Candles and matches have saved me too; they have provided just enough heat to raise the interior temperature in the cabin and keep me from freezing until help finds me. And what does one do in these kinds of situations when one has to take a pee? A bucket or bottle on hand will suffice. The whole ordeal just gets a lot better too, if there are some snacks in the pack to stave off the inevitable hunger pangs.

I proceed to check the contents. An unspoken dialogue plays in my mind as I sort through everything. Thanks, Dad, for the hand-me-down skidoo suit. Here is my face mask with no nose or mouth that makes a white hoarfrost beard when I exhale but keeps my face from freezing. And here's the old, fringed, plaid wool blanket I grew up with when snuggling down in the back seat of the car. I have packets of matches, a huge stubby candle, and a plastic pail to pee in should I need to shelter in my vehicle. Here's the lantern with spare batteries. And most importantly, I have some lunch and a thermos of hot coffee, along with some emergency granola bars. Okay, I think to myself, it looks like I'm good to go.

Still silently engaged in a methodical check, I next do a routine vehicle maintenance check. The gas gauge reads FULL and the headlights and tail lights are working on both sides. I have a windshield scraper, snow brush, and light shovel should I have to dig myself out of a snowbank. The five gallon pail of gravel could help there, too, if I need to get some traction on ice. And, I have my usual extra quart of heavy oil. Fortunately, I won't have need of the jumper cables today, unless it's to rescue somebody else. I will keep the tire iron just behind my feet as it's been a handy defence weapon on more than one occasion. Not every farmer's dog has been a friendly greeter, and coyotes have come a little too close for comfort back on the farm, when getting them out of the hen house or when checking for the whereabouts of newborn calves.

"Okay, got my spare keys, let'er run and lock it," I declare out loud, "and let me get back into that warm office to grab just one more cup of hot coffee before I have to head off to the locker room to get changed into my forestry uniform," I tell myself out loud.

Ready for my work day, I head back out to the truck. As I settle into the driver's seat, I feel a soft, warm heat around my legs at last. I dare to turn on the radio. "Should be no drain on my battery now," I convince myself out loud. "Ahhh," I breathe with a sigh of relief, "I am in contact with the waking world." And I rumble away on four square tires . . . into yet another day of arctic cold . . . into one day closer to my kids.

CRACK!

Crack!—the sound of a rifle. My eyes fly open, bulging wide as if they are coming out of my head. I am frozen in my bed; I know I just heard a gunshot. I lie flat and still, afraid I might get hit by a stray bullet. I am fully awake now and able to collect my thoughts. If that was from a backfiring vehicle, I reason, it would have been a more full-sounding kind of bang. I am certain I heard what sounded like a single gunshot—a sharp, crisp, crack.

The window above my head is open, and I feel the summer night air wafting over me. I now hear the faint sound of male voices, to the west I think, maybe a couple houses down. I lie very still, listening intently. It sounds like they are arguing.

I roll over to the phone on my bedside stand and, with trepidation and keeping my voice down for fear someone will hear me through the open window, I call the Operator. "Hello, is this the Operator? I need help please. I need to talk to the RCMP . . . yes, the Royal Canadian Mounted Police detachment . . . the police, right away," I plead. The Operator immediately patches me through. I am still relaying my information to the RCMP dispatch when I hear their sirens already on the way. The rapidity of the oscillating, piercing shrillness sends chills down my spine. I continue to just lie there after I hang up the phone, still too afraid to move.

I feel an apprehension, a foreboding sense that something bad is about to happen, and I break out in a cold sweat. I am keenly aware that I am alone in the house. My boyfriend had quickly checked in with me yesterday when he got off work, casually smooching me goodbye and laughingly shouting back over his shoulder as he went out the door, "Don't wait up for me, I may pull another all-nighter with the guys." He did that a lot.

Damn! I hate this town, I silently curse to myself. Whatever possessed me to come here, I have wondered many times since moving in with my boyfriend. His lifestyle and our relationship are not as I had imagined. I think back to our coming together as I lie here.

My boyfriend and I met only a month ago at an all-inclusive resort near the city of Matamoros, Mexico. Friends of mine, who have travelled to Mexico, had told me that Canadians my age frequented the resorts' swim-up pool bars in order to meet people. Consequently, anxious to meet a guy and have some fun, I had visited the pool on my very first day of arrival. Almost immediately, I had found myself drawn to a massively muscled and partially submerged male torso sitting at the bar.

Intrigued by his tan, that is, his dark and weathered face, neck, and lower arms against the whiteness of the rest of him, I had determined that it could only mean one thing—that he must be a recent arrival from somewhere up north and was, therefore, likely on vacation and would be around for awhile. How perfect, I had conspired to myself.

Without further ado, I had subtly slipped into the water and deliberately glided across the pool toward him. Upon reaching him, I had deftly pushed myself up and out of the water and had perched on the empty stool beside him.

"Hi, I'm Megan," I had said.

"Merrick," he had replied, readily turning toward me with a grin and handshake. I recall having felt an immediate spark and, for me, he was the epitome of maleness with his rugged outdoor looks, tough and calloused hands, and wildly untamed hair. I had also detected a shyness in his manner which just made him all the more appealing to me. Even our names had seemed to have had a rhythmical ring together: Merrick and Megan. There had been no doubt in my mind that this was my kind of man.

We had started up a conversation, and Merrick had clearly become more and more relaxed as his Coronas disappeared, one by one. "Yah, I'm from High Prairie, a small town about four hours northwest of Edmonton, Alberta," he had said. "I work on the oil rigs up there, ten days in and ten days out of camp. Me and my buddies decided we were badly in need of a break, and so we flew down here to Matamoros to have some fun in the sun—ten glorious days to be exact," he had breathed out slowly with a long, happy sigh of relief. Merrick had gone on introducing himself and, with a puffed up chest, his head held high, and a wide grin, he had boasted "In my spare time, I'm an avid hunter too. Yep, I'll often go out into the bush to snag myself a moose or an elk. Then me and my friends, we carve it up and share the meat. Makes for some great barbecuing." I had been impressed.

With one margarita down and another on the way, I had quickly shared, as well, "Wow, it's really great meeting you! I've just arrived for a two-week vacation. I hope I am going to see a lot more of you." "I'm here with a girlfriend but," I had quickly added "although we're travelling together and sharing a room, we are mostly doing our own thing." "I'm a legal assistant at a law firm in Calgary and, like you, I too, am really in need of a break," I had told him, intentionally emphasizing my availability for a good time.

I had strategically contemplated that overwhelming him with too much personal information all at once would only serve to spoil the ambience of our meeting, and therefore, decided that more could wait for later, if there was to be a later. We had refreshed, from time to time, by sliding our baking bodies into the soothing, velvety, tropical warmth of the water. Mellowed by the effects of the alcohol and the sultry heat around us, we had quickly and fortuitously established what was clearly going to be—a memorable vacation.

At the same time, however, I had found my thoughts frequently interspersed with memories of my past love-life. I had wondered how and when those discussions and disclosures might come up over the next few days. I had recently broken off a long relationship with a live-in partner of more than five years. He had been a reliable and stable sort, but our daily routine and interactions had, at best, been very boring and had only become progressively worse. The relationship had just slowly died, and I was so ready for some life and excitement in a man.

Merrick and I drifted into a blissful blur for the remainder of our vacation. We had congregated with his friends every evening in an atmosphere of fun, food, and fiesta. But sadly, our last night together inevitably arrived.

The mariachi band, that played at the dinner club on our last evening, had attended our table frequently-as if keenly aware of our increasingly intense intimacy. Gently focusing their eyes on Merrick and I, they would approach slowly, sending seductive glances and singing songs of romance. Then their tempo would gradually mount into a crescendo of frenzied passion emanating from their guitars, as they simultaneously whirled the brims of their pure white sombreros, fervently stomped their heels, and flashed the studs of silver that adorned the length of their torso and legs.

Merrick loved to dance. We had been quick studies in learning some of the basic meringue and salsa steps. But on this last night, Merrick had instead, gently swept me away during a waltz routine, across the polished white marble terrace, and into the star-filled night. We had descended the staircase and wound our way along a crushed stone pathway down to the bay where we had cozied into the seclusion of the rocks. There, nestled tightly together as one, we had gazed, in uninterrupted silence, at the fragile, foil-like silver of the moon that floated on the horizon, casting shimmering waves across the water. The tropical night air had been humid and seductively close as its silkiness caressed our skin.

Merrick unexpectedly shifted and, with a swift and strong embrace around my thighs, had lowered my body down onto the sun-warmed sand amidst the rocks. His tallness and firmness had enveloped me, and I had welcomed his seasoned and exploring touch. Merrick had made love to me, slowly, and gently, as if the memory of the moment must last forever. He had wrapped himself around me in the afterglow, and we had drifted into sleep lulled by the lapping of the waves against the rocks.

As the sun rose, we had stirred to the sound of seagulls overhead. Merrick had held me for a very long time, seemingly trying to prolong this moment in time that was infinitely ours. But he had to go. He was scheduled to fly back to Edmonton in the early afternoon.

Earnestly looking into my eyes, his voice quivering and his lips trembling, he had pleaded "Megan, I have to know you will be a part of my life moving forward. I cannot just leave you behind. I need you. You have to tell me you will move up north to be with me. Please, Megan. Promise me you'll start arranging it as soon as you get home. We can work the rest out later."

Without hesitation, I had promised "I will, Merrick. I will follow, I'll move. I want to be with you too. I don't want to let you go."

Within two weeks, I had resigned from my place of employment in Calgary, had packed up my car, and had arrived at High Prairie. It had been a joyful reunion. And Merrick's recent purchase of a fully-renovated bungalow would allow us plenty of room to begin our life together.

My next concern, once I had settled in, had been to find a job. I had set out around town, dressed in my usual, casual, business attire, in order to make professional contacts in person, and to drop off my résumé and references. My first random encounter had been with a middle-aged female, perhaps around fifty years of age, while I had been waiting for the lights to change at an intersection. Her attire, by contrast, seemed to have been that of a woman who had manual labour chores to take care of. She wore a heavily soiled wind and water resistant parka, jeans, and work boots. Her face appeared weathered and lined, and her bare hands were gnarled and calloused. She had looked me up and down and, with a sneer on her lips, had loudly declared for all around to hear, "Looking like that, you're either a hooker, or you don't belong here." I had felt absolutely mortified and appalled! I was stunned! My eyes opened wide with shock. I recovered somewhat and stared back at her in disgust. As the light changed, I had continued on to cross the street-alone.

I had walked about a block before getting to my destination. It had given me time to regroup my thoughts and regain my composure. "What just happened there?" I asked myself as I exhaled loudly. I had been keenly aware of my professional appearance as I had walked along, but in view of why I was dressed like that, it had never occurred to me that the everyday folk on the street would take offence to me. I pondered that, maybe, it was the short skirt or the black pantyhose that I had been wearing. I often wore a dress or skirt at work and, in my mind, the outfit had merely been a typical set of casual business coordinates for me.

Had I triggered something in the woman, I wondered, that had caused her to lash out at me like that. I considered, on the one hand, that maybe my appearance had reminded her that she was tired of who she was or who she had become. Or, on the other hand, maybe my appearance had reminded her that she very much liked who she was and resented someone like me moving into her territory. In any event, it had all certainly been a very shocking and unnerving experience for me.

As I arrived at the first lawyer's office, I had been taking some deep breaths on entering. A receptionist had immediately approached me to ask "Are you alright?" In retrospect, I must have looked somewhat distraught alright. When I recounted my morning to her, she had laughingly replied "Yes, considering it's 1985 now, High Prairie has been a frontier town here in the north for a long time-since the fifties-pretty much since the railway was moved here from Grouard. The presence of a local RCMP detachment, too, is still pretty new here. But actually, things have recently been getting a lot better around here. The town is now considered a major hub with established businesses, modern homes and schools, and people demand a safe and progressive place to live."

My thoughts are suddenly interrupted by the loud and harsh ring of the phone, and I am startled into a sitting position. I glance at the alarm clock and realize that my musings, about how I have ended up in this remote place, must have been going on for over half an hour now. As I fumble with lifting the receiver, I hear an RCMP officer quickly introduce himself saying, "I'm following up with you to confirm that there has been a shooting alright. A man is dead as a result. Are you okay?" he asks.

"Thank you so much for letting me know what is happening," I respond, while breathing a sigh of relief. "I am fine, just alone and scared."

The officer reassuringly tells me "We have things under control. There is nothing for you to worry about. Thank you for calling it in and—if you need anything, just let us know."

Daylight is breaking. I finally feel safe enough to get up and move around. I put on some coffee and make my way to the television. I turn it on and flip to the local news channel.

"*Breaking news!*" announces the broadcaster. "*The local RCMP are reporting a homicide, having occurred at approximately two fifty a.m., the result of a shooting. The police remain on-site and the area is cordoned off. The public are strongly advised to stay away. We will keep you informed as new information becomes available to us.*"

I am worried. Where is Merrick, I frantically ask myself. Why hasn't he called, I wonder. He left almost twelve hours ago. I don't even know who to call to ask about his whereabouts. This is not fair to me, I say to myself, as my temper flares and I begin to fume. I don't like being treated this way, taken advantage of this way. He just takes off, leaving me alone—for hours. He doesn't even call me. I am really angry. "Damn him! He is going to hear from me, once and for all, when he walks through that door. I am not going to be his patsy, not now, not ever!" I curse, and slam a cupboard door.

I remain glued to the television updates. At last, another update is released:

"*According to the latest police reports, three local Caucasian men, known to one another, had congregated at the address now under investigation. Evidence suggests that they had cooked, and shared a meal while seated around the kitchen table. Alcohol was involved. Although the names of the men have not yet been released, they are known to be avid wild game hunters. The rifle used in the shooting has been identified as an All-Purpose All-Star Weatherby Vanguard Series 2, an all-around big-game, .308 calibre bolt gun.*"

Immediately interrupted by yet another *"Breaking news!"* I don't take my eyes off the screen. I see a TV reporter attempting to carry out a live interview, while running after a man who is being led away to an awaiting police cruiser. The man intermittently erupts in slurred verbal outbursts, over his shoulder toward the reporter, yelling *"I'm a witness . . . saw it all, saw everything . . . we're all friends, man . . . we drank too much, way too much . . . we was all braggin' . . . you know . . . stupid shit, about how good we are with the women, and shit . . . that guy that's dead . . . he went too far ya' know, said he'd been fucking our friend's wife for over two years now, still was . . . tha's when they really got into it . . . got physical fast . . . he killed him man, shot him, grabbed a loaded rifle and shot him . . . blew his fuckin' balls off!"*

The police officer now forcibly ushers the man into the backseat of the cruiser while it appears that two other officers attempt to hold off the advancing reporter and onlookers. The cruiser is immediately leaving the scene.

This is all happening just a couple doors down, I remind myself! I can hear commotion out on the street. I feel sick. I wish Merrick would come home. I remind myself that I've been in High Prairie less than two weeks, have no friends here, have no job, and don't even know any of the neighbours. The doorbell rings. Who can that be, I wonder. I'm not even properly dressed yet. I do not want to talk to anyone. I can't think what to do.

Moments go by. The doorbell rings again. I reluctantly move toward the sitting room window where I discreetly look through the sheer curtains. I see an RCMP patrol car parked on the driveway. I see neighbours, standing in their doorways, watching from across the street. I see vehicles slowing as they pass by, curious to see what is happening here.

I make my way to the front entrance and slowly open the door. Two uniformed police constables are standing there. They quietly introduce themselves and ask "May we come in? We need to speak with you." I show them to the sitting room where they remain standing. One of the constables proceeds to tell me that it was him who had called earlier to inform me there had been a shooting. I sit down at their request. "The victim in that shooting," he officially states, "is Merrick Wagner."

I cannot breathe. I cannot think. "No! Not my Merrick!" I scream, as I crumple to the floor in disbelief. I lie there, unable to move. I am numb with shock. After what seems to be an eternity of cognitively swirling confusion and gnashing torment, my brain begins to slowly comprehend the horrific events of these last hours.

I feel cold. I feel empty. I can feel one of the constable's hands on my shoulder. I mechanically lift my head to look at them and tell them "He didn't come home last night. I knew something was wrong, I could feel it."

As both constables crouch down to assist me in getting up, one of them immediately inquires, with an emphatically apologetic tone, "is there anyone we can call for you?"

I get up with robot-like movements. I feel emotionally flat. I feel nothing. I stand motionless in a purposeless stare. My thoughts begin to slowly process like the *tick-tock* of a clock. I pause, and after a deep and soulful sigh, I tell both the constables "No-I just want to leave." I suggest they speak with Merrick's parents for any further information or arrangements, telling them "They only live about an hour north of here. I'm going to immediately start preparing to go back to Calgary."

One of the constables quickly replies "It's okay, Megan. We have a patrol car out there as well. Merrick's parents will have already been told of his accident."

I further advise the constables that I will come by the detachment with my keys for the house before I leave town. They ask to see my Alberta driver's license and request a contact telephone number in Calgary; I comply with their requests. They want assurance that I will be okay. I just stare into space; I hear them leave through the front door.

About an hour later . . . another television update:

"A spokesman for the local police has reported that the homicide victim's entire lower abdominal cavity was 'blown away,' and that the victim had succumbed to the profuse bleeding from the femoral artery. The victim has been identified as Merrick Wagner."

With one step repeatedly in front of the other, I am gathering up my personal belongings. The packing forces me to move. I want to get out of this town-now. I methodically load the suitcases into my car. I call my girlfriend in Calgary. I tell her "Just listen. Don't ask me anything. I'm on my way. We'll talk when I get there." And I promptly hang up. I know there is nothing here for me now, and I realize, there probably never was.

GRIEF . . .

Word has reached me mid-morning that my son has been shot. One of my work colleagues, so emotionally upset that I could hardly make out what she was saying, has just called me to say ". . . there's been a shooting-in Grouard . . . it's your son-he's been shot . . . apparently happened some time yesterday. My parents, they live in Grouard . . . they have a phone . . . they just called me . . . not sure, but I think that's where the shooting happened . . . they could only tell me what they know from rumours that are circulating around the community . . . write this down. I'm going to give you driving directions to where you might find him . . . word has it that he's asking for you . . . I don't know the status of his condition . . . don't know what you'll find when you get there . . . hurry . . . take care . . . call me when you can."

My mind is racing. It will take me at least an hour to get myself organized, fill up with gas, and then drive from here in High Prairie to Grouard. I prepare to leave immediately. I pause to throw together a small emergency first aid bag.

I have not been back to the hamlet of Grouard for years, I think to myself, as I pull on to Highway AB-2 and head east. It is not long before I am passing by the hamlet of Enilda, and I watch for the Highway AB-750 turnoff where I exit to continue driving north. The drive to Grouard is automatically conjuring up thoughts that remain, even to this day, too painful for me. To have continued living in that community after my husband Lucien died would have been more than I could bear. I used to see his familiar, teasing grin and hear his quiet laughter at every turn when I was there.

Lucien was born and had grown up in Grouard. He had never left this community that meant so much to him—the home of his parents long passed, connections with childhood friends, fishing expeditions on Lesser Slave Lake waters, and a laid back lifestyle he felt comfortable in and accustomed to. His work had been seasonal, consisting mostly of odd jobs with local highway maintenance and road construction crews. I recall him complaining, at times, about how monotonous and gruelling, and even potentially dangerous, the work was. But on the other hand, he would argue, the pay was good and at least he could sustain us year-round on his income.

My thoughts drift back to the first time we met, only a few miles out of town. He had been one of the flagmen that day and was directing traffic as I rolled to a full stop alongside him. I remember being so attracted to him. He was a handsomely striking figure, standing slim and tall in yellow bib coveralls, a reflector vest, and heavy work boots. His white t-shirt was a stark contrast against his tan. And his raven-black hair, escaping from beneath his safety helmet, had glistened wet with sweat in the hot sun.

As I rolled down the window to inquire about the road conditions up ahead, it became imminently clear that Lucien's intentions were to make the most of our brief encounter that day.

"Well, hello there! I don't believe I know you. What brings you to this fine neck of the woods today? And where might you be headed to?" he had boldly and determinedly requested to know.

Enamoured of his charismatic ease and personable grin, not to mention his dancing black eyes, I had quickly volunteered "I'll be working as an Educational Technician at the Alberta Vocational College in Grouard. I hope to do some further upgrading while there, as well, in relation to my technician diploma."

"Judging by that accent, I'd say you're not from around these parts," he had said with an inquisitive inflection.

"You are absolutely correct," I had responded, confirming his conjecture. I explained "Although I am of mixed Indigenous ancestry, I am from Syracuse, New York—you are probably hearing my New Yorker broadness. With the economic decline there, I decided to venture out to wherever a job may take me. And, after some random research on this area, and careful consideration, here I am."

I can still see the fleeting look of satisfaction that had passed over his face and how pleased he had seemed to be with our conversational exchange. He had impressed me with how intently he had seemed to absorb my every word.

"Lucien," he had said as our eyes locked. "My name's Lucien," he had proudly stated.

"Madeleine," I had replied back.

With a confident nod, Lucien had announced "I'll be seeing you again. I plan to drop by that college one day very soon to find you. I hope I will get to know you a whole lot better. I'd also like to show you around the area if you will allow me."

As I had driven away, he had flashed me a grin. I had waved back to him and, hoping he could hear me over the road noise, had called out "I will be looking forward to seeing you again, too." At the very least, I had hoped that the smile on my face would have been enough encouragement for him to follow through on his proposal.

A year later, we were married in a quiet ceremony in the small chapel at the college. I was pregnant at the time and, six months later, we became the proud and ecstatic parents of our son, Xavier. Lucien and Xavier were immediately inseparable.

My reminiscing now fast-forwards to a hot day in July, five years later. Xavier and I had been waiting for Lucien to return home from work and walk through the door as he always did. We had planned to fire up the grill that evening for a relaxing, summertime backyard barbecue. But it was getting late, and Lucien still had not come home. He had been working long hours whenever he got the opportunity, always trying to bolster those pay cheques.

I remember having felt so relieved when the company truck finally rolled into our driveway. However, it was not Lucien who got out of the truck, but rather, two men, unknown to me, who had slowly made their way to the house. They were covered in dust and had looked exhausted. I had met them at the door, holding Xavier's hand tightly in mine. They had introduced themselves as Lucien's coworkers and had promptly proceeded to tell me "there's been a terrible accident."

A chill had run through my body as I had desperately searched their eyes for any news of Lucien. I remember how grim their faces had looked, and how they had continuously clenched and unclenched their jaws. They had explained how Lucien had been operating a packer for compressing the freshly-laid asphalt. They recounted how he had stopped to dismount from his machine in order to clear away some debris from in front of the roller. Their explanations had faltered as they tried to clear their throats in their attempts not to cry. One of the men, overcome by a sudden and uncontrollable gasping sob, had beseechingly looked to the other to tell me "The machine just suddenly lurched forward. It pinned Lucien's boot beneath the roller and just kept advancing. Lucien yelled out, but we couldn't reach him in time." Both men's' voices had broken in unison as I heard them say, "Lucien was crushed and killed."

I had felt Xavier's hand go ice cold. I had turned to him, as I buckled to my knees in shock, trying to hold him close. But he had remained stiff and motionless. I saw the light go out of his eyes.

A persistent and pervasive emptiness seemed to consume Xavier after that. He had been a good boy growing up, insisting on completing high school and attending college in Grouard, adamant that he would stay as close to the memory of his father as he could. And so, when I left Grouard at that point, for a career opportunity of my own at the Northern Lakes College in the town of High Prairie, he had gone to live with his friend Remy and parents, Armonde and Josette.

My career path had monopolized my mind and my time, and I had wanted it that way. It gave me a reason to get up each day, a way to move forward with my life, an escape from my consuming grief and persistent depression. It was a substitute to fill the constant void I felt in missing Lucien.

Xavier, too, has been finding his own way through his grieving process. He was now a young man and wanted to hang out with his friends, not his mommy. As a result, we have seemed to slowly distance and grow apart. More than ever, this has all been a time of Xavier's life in which he should have been in the company of his dad, enjoying male bonding times together.

My mind snaps back to the present as I am arriving at Grouard. I turn left off the highway on to Mission St. Not much has changed, but I realize that my memories for detail here have faded and become vague. The place is eerily quiet with not a single person in sight. A feeling of fear creeps over me and I lock my doors. I feel that I am being watched.

I get my bearings once I can see the iconic, original Roman Catholic Mission Church dominantly rising up on a prairie grass knoll and overlooking the town and surrounding landscape. Despite this church's prominent presence in the community, I had always felt such a paradoxical disconnect when I lived here. Instead of a coming-together, in the church for example, by connecting through a common religious affiliation and, perhaps, a camaraderie of related social gatherings, each household always seemed so closed off, to the point of being even suspicious and afraid of the other.

On the one hand, Grouard and area is steeped in a rich history, as well as being proudly credited with the first known alliances between settlers and Indigenous peoples. Reflecting back, the Woodland Cree Indigenous peoples originally inhabited this area. But in 1872, with the establishment of the Roman Catholic Grouard Mission and the colonization that followed, it became a main trading centre on the

Peace River Trail by 1880. Today, Grouard is known as the oldest community in the province of Alberta.

On the other hand, despite that proud history, along with an ever-present guidance from the Roman Catholic Mission Church, it seems to me, that this community has always been, to a large extent, pervaded by contradictory lifestyles of addiction and abuse. That is, every family here seems to have a member who has been permanently injured in some way, usually from an alcohol-driven violent incident. This notion strikes perilously close to my own heart right now as I focus on trying to locate my son and find out what has happened to him.

I have taken more than one erroneous turn as I look for the house in which my colleague told me I might find Xavier. I believe I've finally found it and slowly roll up to the entrance. The area has been well packed from foot traffic in the snow. I become increasingly nervous as I also notice drops of fresh blood in the snow. I see no one, and there are no vehicles parked nearby. The house appears to be an original cabin of this area, constructed of squarely hewn logs, repetitively remodelled and added onto. Over the years, the house appears to have sunk forward into the earth at an angled tilt, giving it the look of a back-in-time, tired, poor man's abode. The small windows are nailed shut. The only evidence of any hominess is from the thin, wispy smoke that rises from a stubby straw and clay-brick chimney.

I grab the emergency bag I had hurriedly packed, and proceed to knock loudly on the vertically planked door. There is no response, and no sign of life. I notice the badly rusted lock that appears to be an old type of steel deadbolt and, as I squint through the cracks in the door, I see on the other side what appears to be a flat, rotating iron bar that lowers into a metal bracket, probably for further reinforcement. The place seems to be fortified, and that is scaring me.

I am frantic, and I pound and pound on the door. After what seems an eternity, I hear a woman's voice. I can see her peering back at me from the other side of the door. She inquires "Who are you?"

I quickly explain "I was told that my son has been injured and that I would find him at this house." She instructs me to wait, and I hear her footsteps retreat as she goes back inside.

The woman returns, but is now accompanied by a male who also peers at me from behind the door. He unlocks the deadbolt, lifts the iron bar, and with difficulty, slowly drags the door open. They look me up and down, and gesture to me to come inside. The man immediately locks and bars the door again.

I seem to be in a kind of a porch. It is a fairly large anteroom with no heat. My eyes slowly adjust to the dim light coming from only a single, suspended electric bulb, but I can see frost glistening on the walls. The floor is strewn with old carpet pieces. I am overcome by a permeating stench of what seems to be motor oil, wet fur, fat, and blood. There are pelts hanging everywhere—skinned rabbits, I think, and maybe the odd fox. Stacked in the corners and around the walls, I see split firewood, grease and oil-stained rags, and splayed and scraped animal carcasses—coyotes, maybe?

The man and woman appear to be a middle-aged Indigenous couple. He now repeats the same process with a second door that seems to lead into the interior of the house. Who and what are these people afraid of, I wonder? As we step into a kitchen, I welcome the blast of heat coming from a wood burning stove. We proceed to sit around the kitchen table, and the couple gently interrogate me further as if to be absolutely certain that I am whom I say I am. They suspiciously ask me a lot of questions about what and who I saw as I drove in. It has been about a half hour of this type of interrogation and my anxiety level is now more than I can bear. In a tone of loud exasperation, I demand "I need to see my son."

Subsequently, a man's head begins to slowly emerge from a lifting cellar trap door beside my chair. I am terrified. He appears to be Indigenous as well, and about my son's age.

"It's Remy!" I blurt out in surprise. I had not recognized him. He has changed so much since I last saw him. I now turn back to look at the middle-aged couple and stare at them for several seconds. Although barely audible, I declare "Armonde and Josette!" I had not recognized them either. Remy nervously interjects to tell me "Xavier is down in the cellar. I'll take you down to see him."

We immediately descend on steep, wooden ladder steps. The cellar smells earthy and damp, and I feel a chill. It, too, is dimly lit by a single, suspended electric bulb.

"Hi Mom," a weak and worried sounding voice calls out. It's Xavier, lying on a spring cot and covered with blankets and an old buffalo robe. He looks pale and is grimacing at times. I rush to hold him.

Remy quickly explains their current situation to me. "Xavier and I-well, we moved out of my parents' place-you know, Armonde and Josette's, some time ago-after we dropped out of college," he confesses, his hands nervously fidgeting and his eyes lowering as if afraid to tell me. I am so obviously disappointed, so very disappointed to hear this. I have had such high aspirations for Xavier upon completing college. I should have known about this. "We've been living in this cabin that had belonged to my grandparents," Remy goes on. "We wanted to have our own place, feel more grownup, you know, do our own thing. I guess things have been kind of getting out of control though. There isn't much to do around here, we never have any money, and we've been drinking a lot—a lot," he admits and casts his eyes downward again.

Remy's conversation now revolves around the activities that have led up to Xavier's injury. Appearing both scared and ashamed, he tells me "We have been bootlegging. That's how we make some money for ourselves-selling liquor, and sometimes pills, to the underage kids here in Grouard and surrounding area."

His face appears ashen in the dim light as he excitedly relays the rest of the story to me. He goes on to explain "Well, things went real bad this time. There was an ugly confrontation during our planned meetup with some kids. Things escalated and turned into a brawl-everybody fighting. One of the junior high students, that we regularly sell to, started waving a handgun around and it accidentally went off, shooting Xavier in the leg, the front of his left thigh. Everyone got scared and took off, but I stayed to help Xavier. He was in a lot of pain and really bleeding bad; he couldn't walk by himself. So I helped him hobble back to our cabin. We were scared about what the cops might to do us if they found out about this. So, I helped Xavier get down the ladder into the cellar in order to hide him there. Then, I ran to my parents' place to get help." I am struggling to process everything that has happened, while at the same time, assess Xavier's condition. I determine it is now about fifteen hours since the shooting happened.

I gently pull the robe and blankets away from Xavier's leg. His jeans have been removed.

After Armonde and Josette had arrived, I am told that Josette had immediately washed Xavier's injured leg, had cleaned and doused the wound with a birch tree bark tincture to alleviate the pain, and then had packed it with a sphagnum moss wad to stop the bleeding. She had next wrapped the leg in clean rag strips to secure the moss and to help absorb any further bleeding.

Xavier is very pale, probably due to having lost a lot of blood in his attempt to get to the cabin, and I can see that the bandaging is soaked through, as well. I tell him "I'm coming back to change that bandage, but first, I need to talk to Armonde, Josette, and Remy about getting you to a doctor." Remy and Xavier look scared. They apparently still do not want anyone to know about all this as they do not want trouble with the police.

Just then, Armonde shouts down that Josette has prepared a light meal for us. Remy and I climb up the stairs but I quickly turn the conversation to Xavier's immediate need for medical care. The weather has been steadily deteriorating since noon, and we are now completely engulfed by the fury of a blizzard. Armonde turns on the radio in the kitchen, and an emergency weather bulletin is reporting zero visibility and advising everyone to stay off the roads, and to not abandon their vehicles should they currently be caught in the storm. I come to the grim realization that we will not be going anywhere for the time being.

I have been so preoccupied with getting here, and have felt so distraught, that thoughts of food have been the furthest thing from my mind. However, as I smell the faint aroma of a fresh, hot, unleavened bread, and the steeping scent of sage, my hunger pangs are aroused. We all sit around the kitchen table to hurriedly share a plate of dried salt whitefish, lightly smoked and dried moose meat jerky, along with some fry bread. I quickly wash it down with the herbal tea that Josette tells me she makes from berries and sage she had picked and dried during the summer months.

Josette also gives me some boiled meat and fish broth, along with some herbal tea for Xavier. I hurriedly descend into the cellar again, and attempt to spoon sips of broth into him. We nervously chat about anything that comes to mind.

Xavier complains of feeling cold, but his skin is getting hot to the touch. I change his bandage, but this time I use the items I brought with me. I clean the area with alcohol and pour hydrogen peroxide into the wound which should serve both as an antibacterial, as well as, an effervescent to remove any debris. However, I am careful, as I don't want to dislodge the clotting and start the bleeding again. I squeeze a tube of triple antibiotic ointment into the wound, apply four by four inch gauze squares, top those with sterile absorbent pads, and loosely wrap his thigh with rolled gauze. The bleeding is minimal.

Eleven p.m. Twenty-four hours now since the shooting. I wrap myself in a blanket, seat myself beside Xavier, and hold his hand and talk to him. He feels very hot. He is mumbling and is now incoherent at times. I keep offering him sips of warm tea. He is peeing, but not much, and it is concentrated in colour and smells strong. I think he is severely dehydrated and, perhaps becoming septic. I go back upstairs to turn on the radio. The weather report advises that the storm will not begin to subside until early morning.

I return to the cellar and, pulling my chair up beside Xavier, lay my head by his chest. I begin to doze but continuously hold his hand, counting down the hours one by one.

Five a.m. Xavier is burning up. He is delirious, and not making any sense. I go up to the kitchen and turn on the radio for another weather update. The storm is beginning to subside. It sounds to me like the wind has gone down outside. I call out "Hey-everybody—hey, wake up!" Armonde, Josette, and Remy emerge and we again gather around the kitchen table. Josette gets up and begins making bannock and coffee while we talk. She serves it with her homemade wild strawberry and gooseberry jams as I frantically tell them "the radio report has advised that all highways and roads are now impassable, blown in with hard-packed snow, and that the plows are not expected to be out until after noon. Xavier is bad; he's burning up, delirious. We can't wait any longer to get him to a hospital." The sober and worried expressions on our faces say it all.

Remy promptly stands up and determinedly proposes "We need to make an immediate exit plan. I'll work something out. Start getting him ready. We need to get him to a hospital. We'll take him to High Prairie."

I immediately go back down to the cellar in order to change Xavier's bandage again. I have used all the supplies I brought with me and resort to Josette's remedies: the bark tincture, moss packing, and clean rags. I can no longer make my son drink. His tongue and lips are parched and cracked. I wipe on some lard that Josette has brought me.

Seven a.m. Faint daylight. The storm has subsided. Remy has clambered through the snowdrifts to a neighbour's shack just yards away. They have skidoos. The men hook two of them to a stone boat on skids and bring it around to Xavier and Remy's porch entrance.

We swaddle Xavier in the buffalo robe, wrap him with blankets, and secure everything with ropes. The men then hoist my son up and out of the cellar. They carry him outside and place him, feet first, onto the stone boat. I dress as warm as I can, and sit spread eagle on the back of it with my son's head in my lap, and hang on to the rope handles on the side.

Eight a.m. Remy and one of the neighbour friends rev up the skidoo motors, and we set off. Remy has advised that we will not take the highways in order to save time but will, instead, travel diagonally across country toward High Prairie. Thankfully, the heaviness of the stone boat on skids, along with the combined weights of both Xavier and myself, allows for a consistent and easy passage through the heavy snowdrifts.

Nine thirty a.m. We are in town limits, and I can see the hospital up ahead. I cannot feel my hands and feet. I don't think Xavier is conscious. Remy and his friend glide us into the Emergency driveway. As they jump from their machines, staff are already arriving with a stretcher. They lift Xavier onto it, and he quickly disappears from my view. I am assisted into a wheelchair as I cannot feel my hands and feet.

Ten a.m. I relay an account of what I know to a nurse in Admitting.

Eleven a.m. Thirty-six hours now since the shooting. A doctor approaches and wheels me to Xavier's side in the Emergency ward. They have placed him on a warming blanket. Intravenous infusions are dripping, along with attached mini bags of medication. He has a urinary catheter attached to a drainage bag, and he is hooked up to beeping cardiac and vital sign monitors. There is a flurry of activity with staff coming and going to take blood specimens, and to keep checking everything.

My mind is racing as I try to process so many thoughts about my son's last months. I fear I am too late. My son had needed me. I should have been visiting my son frequently, staying abreast of what was happening with him. I feel I have failed him terribly. He's made some bad choices. Heavy drinking and getting involved in alcohol related activities was not the answer to his problems.

Why did he drop out of college, I wonder. He's a smart boy. Maybe he was just bored with his life in Grouard and was merely looking for some excitement, a break from a mundane, daily routine of going to school. Or, I contemplate, maybe he was led astray by Remy and some others. I think too, that he could have been depressed, not unlike me, in attempting to find his way through the grieving process. Did he feel that alone, I wonder. I wish he had talked to me, that I had regularly reached out to him. This is my fault. I know how much he missed his dad.

I consider too, that maybe it was the drinking that had changed him. Maybe, there were times when he was too hung over to go to school, that is, felt too sick to go to class. It goes without saying, as well, that he was probably not eating properly either. Maybe the alcohol temporarily made him feel better about things, about himself. But if it did, I think to myself, was he finding himself more and more alienated as a result of it, that is, losing friends because of it and getting caught up, instead, with a bad crowd. It is clear to me that Xavier has been in a downward spiral of events and coping strategies for some time.

The doctor quietly approaches Xavier's stretcher. Gently placing his hand on my shoulder, he tells me "Xavier is in septic shock. He may not live." I feel numb. I request a priest to administer the sacrament of last rites.

I hold my son close and keep whispering "I love you," in his ear. I feel his body go limp. He is gone.

I stay with Xavier for a long time . . . in a state of disbelief . . . unable to let go . . . overcome by guilt . . . immobilized by grief. I am not able to come to terms with the harsh and penetrating reality that, indirectly, my son Xavier, has succumbed to alcohol and substance abuse related events.

LENA

Now those are red lips! A deliberate, voluptuous, voluminous application of Ruby Red. How odd, how very, very odd, I think to myself, as this otherwise very plain, middle-aged woman approaches my table to take my order. I am utterly distracted by her appearance, and preoccupied with taking her in from head to toe as she chatters away at me.

Based on my experience, having come from Ontario, this woman appears to me to be dressed in traditional German Mennonite garb and, in all likelihood, is of Old Colony Mennonite descent. She is wearing a home-sewn pastel cotton print frock that is tied at the back with a bow, has a high-cut, plain round neckline, long sleeves, and a hem that falls to mid-calf. Visible from beneath the hem are heavy gauge white stockings and black oxford tie shoes. In other words, her body is most modestly covered. Over her skirt, she has tied a white linen apron that appears to be the property of the restaurant establishment. Her ash-blonde hair, turning grey at the temples, is neatly swept up and rolled around her face and head. A triangular head scarf, matching the pastel cotton print of her dress, is secured neatly in place at the nape of her neck.

I am still attempting to regain my composure when she introduces herself to me. She speaks in broken English, and I can hear what I believe to be a Ukrainian accent. She tells me that her name is Lena, and that is what she likes to be called. Lena further explains that her name is actually Helen, a biblical name meaning "shining light." Well, I think to myself, with those red lips, one can certainly see her coming! Lena continues to laugh and chat away, completely engaged in our interaction and commanding my attention with her constant eye contact. I, on the other hand, seem to be merely gaping at her as I find myself most intrigued by this woman.

"Hi, how are you?" Lena asks, smiling kindly. "I don't think I see you here before-at the grill, I mean. Are you new to here?" she inquires. "Tell me-where you from? Why you here?" she questions, leaning in with curiosity.

Feeling hesitant to so readily disclose my personal information, I briefly reply "Hello to you, too. I've just flown into Edmonton from Toronto. And, I'm going to head north now, to just past Red Earth Creek in order to locate my brother regarding some family matters."

Lena goes on to say "I notice you soon as you pull in, 'cause you park right beside where I park. I right beside you. I drive that old van-all rusty, and the roof, it cave in. And there's like big star cracks where the windshield broke."

I do recall that vehicle as something about it had particularly stood out in my mind. There was a shiny, gold, ornate figurine affixed to the dashboard and ornamental trinkets dangling from the rear view mirror. Considering that she is of probable traditional German Mennonite background, I find myself surprised at her decorative style, not to mention the fact that she actually drives.

Where does this woman comes from, I wonder? I remain perplexed about so many things—her use of lipstick, the ornamentations in her vehicle, her operation of a vehicle, her employment outside of a colony. And why would she be here, working in this remote, northern town? My food has arrived, and Lena leaves me to enjoy it in peace. However, my mind continues to wander and obsess about who this woman is.

As I eat my dinner in silence, I consider that I have known of many German Mennonite colonies in Ontario. I also come to the realization that I have always been of the understanding that, around the late 1800's, many Dutch and north German Mennonites had migrated via Russia and Ukraine to predominantly settle in southern Manitoba. I know, too, that over time, many of the traditionalists apparently moved on to Mexico in a segregating attempt to preserve and maintain their "Old Order" lifestyle. However, due to land scarcity and subsequent economic limitations in Mexico, many had to once again return to various locations in Canada. Maybe Lena is from Mexico, I speculate.

I clearly observe by now that Lena is an industrious and organized worker, and one who pays a great deal of attention to detail. I perceive, too, that she may be just a little bit nosy. Oh well, I rationalize, her ultimate intention seems to be to help if she can, and I certainly respect and value that in a person.

I just seem to have more and more questions about Lena as I continue to ponder about who she is and where she has come from. Is she a woman alone, I wonder? Maybe, she has left her colony, as this is Sunday and she is not in church at a service or communal gathering. A part of her identity, as in her manner of dress, seems to still hold on to traditional ways, while yet another part of her, seems to be breaking away. It's as if she is transitioning to discover the independent woman that she can be in the outside world.

As my imagination runs wild, I continue to fabricate scenarios about who Lena is as a person. I contemplate that perhaps she is merely wayward and somewhat lost with her life. I speculate, too, considering the oddity of all that lipstick, that she could be caught up in a societal role that, although not looked upon by some as acceptable, could perhaps be a lucrative source of income for her. That is, perhaps she is attracting and providing a much sought-after service for certain clients in this transient and isolated town and community. And finally, I consider that maybe Lena is happily aligned with a partner, one who is not from her cultural background, and that she is merely a delightful mix of the best of both her worlds. In any event, I conclude, she certainly seems to be a happy person.

Lena returns to my table, sliding onto the chair across from me. "Mind if I sit here with you? I like your company and I need my break," she confides. "Been on my feet all morning."

I must admit that I find her unreserved spontaneity a little surprising, but I also quite enjoy her friendly and relaxed style. I smile and nod, as if to say I am okay with it.

Lena looks directly into my eyes and, with a determined seriousness, unexpectedly leans forward, placing her hand firmly over mine, and shares "I fifty years old now, but I do okay for myself here in High Prairie. I so very grateful to proprietor and owner of this restaurant. He give me steady work. I have money now. I meet a lot of people, and I make friends here. Here is where I stay."

Taking hardly enough time to regroup for her next train of thought, Lena proceeds to fill me in on what's up in town, who's who, the history of the owner, the grill, the town and, I feel certain, everyone in it. And it doesn't stop there. She seems to know the goings-on for miles around.

My mind is racing as I listen. Lena is, to my way of thinking, an odd fit in the community. But, I notice, she is quick to catch on to things. She misses nothing. Despite her probable humble origins, this woman strikes me as being street smart, loyal, full of grit, and mentally strong. I find her frankness to be unabashedly direct; that is, what you see is what you get. For that reason, I like her and I trust her.

In view of my current circumstances, I know how much I need the assistance of a local friend like Lena. I realize what a valuable resource person she could be for me, someone from whom I can glean all kinds of helpful information. I expect I would also always be able to make contact with her, here at the restaurant and, conveniently too, the motor inn and grill can provide all the essential services I would need if passing through the town of High Prairie on any future trips. I am keenly aware, as well, that I am a woman, travelling alone. In my precarious position of being new to the area and unfamiliar with the ways of this remote territory and the Indigenous peoples around me, I readily acknowledge that I need all the help and support I can get.

I unreservedly commit to giving Lena my undivided attention as I openly seek and accept her support. And I do not hesitate to let her know how much I value her many tidbits of information. I am quick to jot down things like driving directions, timelines, distances, where to locate what I need, inside information, and local tips about key contact persons in the different communities and settlements. I can tell, too, that it makes Lena feel needed and important.

I know I will forever be grateful for having met this woman. I have found an unlikely friend in an unlikely place.

BLOOD ON THE SNOW

To say that he is estranged is putting it mildly. My brother, Adam, had struck out on his own when he was just eighteen. My dad did his best to make a home for us and to keep us together as a family after my mother left when we were still in elementary school. As the older sister and perhaps because I was a girl, my dad and I seemed to bond more comfortably and were better able to maintain a harmonious household. Unfortunately, Dad and Adam were always a contentious duo. It is more than twenty years since I have had any contact with Adam.

However, I believe it is essential to attempt to find him now, as our dad passed over a year and a half ago. Adam should know, and there are personal items of Dad's that I think he should have and will want. There is the matter, too, of settling our dad's estate. He never had much to spare while he was alive, but he was a responsible man and consistently worked hard to pay the bills, feed and clothe us, and keep a roof over our heads. Dad left a will in which his assets—the house, his car, his pension, and the benefits from his life insurance policy—were evenly divided between Adam and myself.

I started my search for my brother by making contact with a girl-friend he'd had at the time of his departure. She is married now with a family of her own, but she still lives in the area. I found her to be most receptive and understanding with regard to my request for help in finding Adam. She told me they had communicated with each another for only about six months after he left. Apparently, he had been working his way across Canada by picking up general labour jobs, and his ultimate plan had been to head to Peace River Country in Alberta. She told me that in his last communication with her, he had mentioned that he would probably travel through the towns of Slave Lake and High Prairie as his prospects for work might be better there. She did not know, however, if that plan had ever materialized, nor of his current whereabouts.

I immediately reported these findings to my dad's lawyer's office. Fortunately for us, Adam had followed through with his plan, and the investigative team had been able to quickly determine his exact whereabouts, a Red Earth Creek address. I booked a flight from Toronto to Edmonton and, upon arrival, rented a small 4WD Ford truck from a rental company at the airport in order to complete the rest of the trip. I have been realistic enough to anticipate difficulty on this venture, but I also firmly believe that I will find Adam. Hopefully, we will reunite as a family and get to a better place with our relationship.

It is now the day after I arrived in Edmonton, and with the early morning skyline behind me, I begin to relax and enjoy the drive. I am heading north and west into Athabasca country on Highway AB-2. The first hour and a half takes me through countryside that is relatively flat with numerous bluffs of trees, though it is mostly cleared for agricultural purposes.

The next three hours of driving turn into a boreal landscape of dense forest comprised of various types of conifers, in particular evergreen pine trees. The air is rejuvenating and fresh. Barks are proliferate with lichens, moss, and fungi. Signs are becoming more frequent, alerting to moose and deer crossings. And I find I am now often having to surrender to the wide and extended loads of logging trucks as well.

As I approach Lesser Slave Lake, driving along the shoreline highway, I can see the vast body of grey, wind-swept water. The lake appears to be surrounded by miles of naturally sandy and wildly overgrown beaches.

I recall having learned about this lake and the surrounding area in elementary school. It's strange, I contemplate, how things one had thought would never matter in life suddenly become relevant. I also recall being taught that the earliest non-Indigenous people had settled here, first with a NW trading post, and next, a Roman Catholic Church Mission.

Although Highway AB-67 (relabelled as AB-88 in 1988) appears to be the most direct route to Red Earth Creek from Slave Lake, I have decided to follow the same route that I believe my brother took, in the hopes of encountering a chance meetup with anyone along the way who may know of him, or perhaps, his exact whereabouts. I continue to drive west on Highway AB-2, heading for the town of High Prairie.

I notice, over the next hour, that I seem to be leaving the forest behind me. The area gradually turns into scruffy brush and dry prairie grassland. I drive through and past several small hamlets, finally arriving in High Prairie where I pull into a full-service rest stop called the Borealis Motor Inn and Grill. I desperately need to stretch my legs, freshen up, and have something to eat. I will fill up with gas before I continue north from here. Having already calculated the approximate driving times according to my maps, I excitedly anticipate being able to locate Adam by suppertime, or at least by early evening.

The motor inn restaurant is quiet, and the proprietor is chatty as he shows me to a table.

"Good afternoon, come right this way please. You travelling alone Miss," he asks with a querying tone. "Will there be anyone else joining you for lunch today?" he further clarifies.

"Thanks for asking, but No," I confirm, "it will just be me for lunch."

"So what brings you to town?" he wants to know. "I merely ask because I haven't seen you come through my restaurant before."

"I flew in from Toronto arriving to Edmonton, where I rented a vehicle to complete the rest of my trip," I reply. Eagerly, I share "I'm hoping to locate my brother, who I think is probably living just north of here, maybe around the Red Earth Creek/Loon Lake First Nations Settlement junction," feeling certain my finding him can't be that far off now.

"Have you ever been up in this part of the country before?" he asks, sounding concerned and watching me intently.

"No," I reply.

"Then you have gone as far as you're going to go for one day," he sternly advises. "It will be getting late by the time you are ready to leave here, and I am telling you that those roads are not any place to be, for a young woman unfamiliar with the area, and travelling alone in the cold and dark. You had better find a place to stay for the night. Leave early in the morning, after you've had some rest, and drive in daylight. I urge you to think about what I've said while you enjoy your meal. I can direct you to a couple places for accommodations if you would like but, of course, we'd be happy to have you stay right here at the Motor Inn."

I feel crushed, and for the first time, even afraid. However, realizing I am probably coming off as somewhat of a naive city gal, I decide to heed his warning, and do as he suggests.

The next morning is dismal, cold, and grey as I backtrack eastward on Highway AB-2 before turning north just past the hamlet of Enilda, and on to Highway AB-750. I am well-rested and, once again, feel optimistic that this will be the day I meet up with my brother. Once I am past the Grouard Mission turnoff, it is not long before I become acutely aware that I am driving in muskeg country. I had read about this while still back in Ontario. The low lying marshy bogs are emitting a particularly dense, wet fog this morning, and the swamp gas is pungently strong. I can barely see the front of the hood of the truck, despite the constant sweep of the wiper blades. I have the defrost settings as high as they will go and I slow to a crawl.

It is still very early in the morning, but company gas and oil trucks are already zooming past me. It seems to me they must know these roads awfully well, considering the severely limited visibility and the speed at which they are going.

I have just driven down through a hollow and am coming up over the crest of a small rise when I slam on the brake. "What the hell!" I blurt out. My vehicle goes into a skid before coming to a complete standstill.

Two enormous, upside-down butt cheeks, with four hoofed legs, and one enormous penis, projecting straight up into the air, lie directly in front of my vehicle. It's a dead horse, and obviously, a gelding. My heart is pounding. My hands are white-knuckled around the steering wheel. I take a big breath in, gradually regain my composure, and slowly breathe out. I speculate that in view of the current positioning of the horse, there have probably already been several hours of decomposition and release of body gases, which would explain the bloating and rigor mortis that I see. I suspect that someone had hit the horse with a vehicle in the fog and dark of night.

I feel such an overwhelming sadness at the loss of such a beautiful animal, and at the thought that the horse may have suffered terribly while dying. However, there is nothing I can do for it now. I also feel certain that previous passers-by will have already reported this mishap.

With my palms still sweating and my heart still racing, I carefully back up in order to pull around the dead animal. I continue north, passing through the more recent acreage developments of the Salt Prairie homesteads. Some appear to be very modern and contemporary with natural wood exteriors while others are an assortment of trailer homes and modest bungalows.

As I continue in a north-easterly direction over the next hour, still on Highway AB-750, the forest becomes sparse and scrappy. The scattering of homes along the road or in the clearings appear impoverished and poorly maintained. I pass through what appears to be the well-established but small and economically depressed Gift Lake Metis Settlement. Considering this would usually be a busy time of morning in most industrious communities, there is no evidence in this settlement of any activity or of anyone visibly out and about. It feels eerily unsettling, and I do not stop.

I continue northeast for about another half hour, arriving at the Atikameg Indigenous Community situated on the northwestern shore of Utikoomak, also known as Utikuma Lake. According to one of the pamphlets I had been skimming before falling asleep last night, Atikameg means Little Whitefish in the Woodland Cree language. On my right is old, faded signage that suggests a past Hudson's Bay Trading Post had once been at this site. While having dinner at the restaurant last evening, I remember overhearing a conversation at a nearby table that could perhaps have been referring to this very site. The gist of that conversation related that, about five years previously, a Hudson's Bay store manager and his wife had both been murdered in Atikameg, and that the authorities had never found who had killed them. This might be where that happened, I think to myself. I panic, and quickly check my doors to be sure they are locked.

I wonder, too, if Atikameg could also be the 1889-1896 Whitefish Lake Post I had read about in the pamphlet at the motel. This community, too, is scattered about, and appears desolate and economically depressed. I am feeling despondent, and by now am even wondering if I am on the right road. It does not seem feasible to me that my brother would live in such an area.

The day continues to be grey, windy, and cold. A light cover of fresh snow has fallen and I follow the road as best I can. However, I am really having difficulty hanging on to the steering wheel on these rough roads. The season is officially spring now, and the permafrost has begun to evaporate. I realize that travelling in this area, in such a small truck, will become increasingly problematic as the muskeg softens. The logging trucks and oil crews have churned up deep ruts, and I am bouncing all over the place.

Without warning, a logging truck—maintaining its speed in order to get its load through on the ever-increasingly unreliable roads—is passing on my left. A BANG! explodes at the left side of my head. I reactively jerk the steering wheel to the right which causes me to veer off the hard-packed road and down onto the thawing muskeg. I feel the truck sink and slow to a labouring crawl as the whining motor tries to chew the vehicle forward. I dare not stop; I clutch down into low gear while keeping my foot depressed hard on the gas pedal.

I glance over at my driver's side window. It is smashed, splintered into a starburst pattern which has become no more than an unstable mesh of in-and-out, sucking glass. The tandem tires of the logging truck have obviously thrown a rock. I am lucky not to have been killed.

A foghorn blast coming from the trucker's horn startles me. He must have seen me veer off the road and has now slowed enough to be driving alongside of me. I can hardly see through the smashed window and flying mud, but he appears to be giving me a thumbs up, along with a big, wide grin, as if to be saying, "Hang in there girl! You're doin' it!"

I am irate. I feel like crying. I feel an erupting, surging urge to, despite all odds, get my little truck back up on that road rather than concede to this guy and his big rig. So there, I angrily think to myself, let the truckers talk about that tonight over their dinner stop!

The trucker stays with me for quite some distance as I churn through the muck. He then briefly toots his horn, and I can see him repetitively pointing at something ahead. I lean forward into the steering wheel, squinting my eyes. I see a large gravelled area ahead that I will be able to drive onto and then pull to the left in order to hopefully get myself back on the hard-packed road.

The trucker speeds ahead of me. I go for it, and I make it! I am back on the packed surface. I can hear him honking and honking, and see him blinking all his back lights. I flash my bright beam headlights in return, and he accelerates into the distance.

My truck, however, is making a terrible racket and is sounding more like a tractor. It seems, too, as if the motor has no guts and is slowly dying. I am pressing the gas pedal to the floor but am barely able to go fifteen miles per hour. I have not gone far when fortuitously, I see a huge sign advertising a wheel and tire service shop located at the upcoming major intersection, northbound to Red Earth Creek and Loon Lake Indigenous Settlement via the adjoining Highway AB-67 (relabelled AB-88 in 1988), and westbound to the town of Peace River. They should be able to help me, I desperately think to myself. At long last—there it is! My truck has made it. I make a rolling right exit into the single hydraulic bay, and get out to look under my truck. The whole exhaust system is hanging and dragging.

A man, covered from head to toe in black grease and wiping his black nails on a greasy rag, smirks his way toward me. Upon looking me over, he just snorts and laughs. Are you kidding me, I choke back. I glare at him. I want to scream. It is now getting well into the afternoon.

I curtly ask him "Can you give me some idea as to when this can be fixed?"

He gets a little more serious, looks things over, asks me a few questions about what happened, and then, shrugging his shoulders, says "I dunno. If you're lucky, I'll be able to get some parts piggy-backed on a trucker's load, maybe later tomorrow or," still shrugging his shoulders, "it could take a couple of days."

I feel like the bottom of my stomach has just dropped out. I am really beginning to question my judgment and doubt my capacity to have tried such a trip. Despondent and angry, I curse under my breath "What a mess!" I cannot imagine there will be anything left of this truck when it comes time to return it to the rental agency in Edmonton. I imagine that it will not take much of an inspection for me to be presented with an assessment amounting to the cost of a brand new vehicle. God, I hope the insurance is going to cover all this, I silently implore.

I resign myself to the fact that I have no choice but to wait and see this through. I am going nowhere fast, and feel absolutely powerless. The operator's newly apologetic tone seems to suggest that perhaps he does feel kind of sorry for me. But his smirk persists as he casts his eyes downward and slyly to the side.

"I'd be more'n happy to let ya' bunk in at my place for the night or—for as long as the parts will take," he offers.

I indignantly decline. I settle instead, for his alternative offer: that he can lock me in the shop that night after he closes. At least I know I'll have access to the adjoining, but filthy restroom with both a sink and a toilet. I proceed to retrieve what snacks I can bang out of the vending machine. Closing time comes, and I curl up for the night on the cracked vinyl sofa from which the foam and stuffing are protruding.

Early the next morning, the operator returns, and by noon, we know that parts are on their way, piggy-backed on a trucker's load. No sooner than we learn that news, the truck arrives. With the help of a mechanic who is a personal friend of the operator's, my truck is repaired and roadworthy again by late afternoon. They have installed a whole new exhaust system and have also replaced the alternator. They have duct-taped the shattered driver's side window as well.

I gas up, check the oil, buy another extra quart, replenish the window washer fluid, wash the windows, shake off the mounds of dried mud from the driver's mat, check that the spare tire and rim are still there, and at long last, I am ready to head north once again. It's a hefty bill but, I truly thank them both from the bottom of my heart. My plan is to reach the Red Earth Creek/Loon Lake Indigenous Settlement Junction before dark.

As I drive away and the Atikameg Community fades into the distance, I am struck by the contrasting and breathtakingly beautiful scenery that surrounds me now. Shafts of sunlight break through the thinning trees and dart across the connecting lakes and ponds. I pull over for a while onto a bed of thick, frozen wetland grass. I can hear the forlorn call of a loon. Muskrats are at play, and grazing elk, deer, and even a moose pause to drink at water's edge. This panorama of pristine stillness in nature is undoubtedly the beauty of the north, so untouched by the noise and pollution of urban industrialization and commercialism.

Regretfully, I can not linger long and soon pull back onto the hardened road and drive on. Within minutes, I have arrived at the junction. On the west side of the highway is Loon Lake, an administrative Indigenous Settlement, and on the east side, Red Earth Creek, a bustling, commercial settler town, smelling of oil, lumber, and money. It has apparently become a town overnight with instant schools and families. I know I will be able to overnight here. I desperately need to unwind. A shower, a change of clothes, a decent meal, and a good night's rest will, I expect, do wonders.

I am soon turning the key in the door of my mobile trailer motel room. I step into a warm, clean, full bathroom accommodation, and momentarily sink into a comfortable chair, trying to comprehend all that has happened over the last hours. I slowly shed my layers of sweat and soil to bask in a warm, steamy, soothing shower spray. Then I quickly refresh, throw on some clean clothes, and head for the adjoining mobile dining kitchen before it closes.

Upon entering the dining room, I am gallantly greeted by two exuberant Lebanese cooks who wave me toward the table at which I should seat myself. I have no sooner pulled up my chair than they appear at my side to serve me their aromatic homemade soup and fluffy, fresh out-of-the-oven flat breads—delicious, absolutely delicious!

The truckers, too, are friendly, politely nodding as they walk past my table. I notice that I am the only woman in the place. They lean over from time to time, attempting to include me in their chit-chat.

In response to their inquiries, I share that I am trying to locate my brother just north of here and, although highly improbable, hope someone may know of him. "Weather's changing," they respond, and with awkward and clumsy invites, assure me there is room to stay with them in their bunk trailers; that is, if I don't feel good about driving on. I thank them very much, but assure them I already have comfortable accommodations.

I retire early without remembering even having laid my head on the pillow. At daybreak, I am awakened by the aroma of coffee wafting through the trailers, the sound of shower pipes banging in the walls, and the camaraderie of the crews as they prepare to head out for the day.

I feel much more optimistic as I set out today. Based on the information and directions the lawyer's office have given me with regard to Adam's location, I must be getting very close. I leave the bustle of the morning activities at the junction behind and continue north, albeit slowly and with great care, as I do not want to miss the correct turnoff. There are no signs, and I am relying solely on the precision of the odometer, carefully gauging my distance in miles from the town limits behind me. However, a niggling, silent skepticism pervades. At one point, I just come out and say it: "What are the odds of me finding him?"

Every turn looks the same as I peer ahead into the seemingly endless oblivion of dark, dense, boreal forest. I have to keep my wits about me, or I will easily miss the turn. The odometer reading finally indicates that this trail on the left must be it. I turn west.

It is ominously quiet as I drive into the trail's darkness, under the canopy of pine boughs overhead, and onto a carpet of conifer cones and needles. I have never experienced this kind of surreal peace and quiet before. The air smells so fresh and clean, and is so untouched by humankind.

I can see a lone male figure in the distance. He has emerged from the forest and appears to be Indigenous with long, coarse black hair tied at the nape of his neck. As I get closer, I see he is dressed in a heavy wool plaid jacket, jeans, and mukluks, and is carrying a small game rifle. In the other hand he has a collection of dead rabbits, each suspended by a hind leg from a leather cord. I wonder if he has been checking his trap lines.

I roll down my driver's side window and yell across the road "I'm trying to locate my brother's place and think it should be on this road. Are you familiar with the people around here?"

The man does not look at me, but rather, with his eyes cast downward, pauses for a long while, and then responds with an abrupt "Ye-uh. I figure there's a trapper-down there," and he waves his arm toward the distant road.

"How far?" I ask.

He replies with another abrupt "Ye-uh. It's pretty far."

"How far?" I press.

"'Til when the sun will be high in the sky," he replies in earnest.

"Will there be any landmarks, anything I can watch for?" I ask, my patience wearing thin. I wonder if this man can possibly know what I have been through to get here. I need him to give me clearer directions.

With the same ambiguity, to my mind, he replies "Ye-uh. There'll be a big rock, and there's a tree with a branch like a big finger. Turn in there. When you can't go no more, you will be there."

I thank him and drive on another three miles. The landmarks were as the man said they would be.

I can now see a south-exposure log cabin, about a hundred yards away, perched on a snow-covered meadow rise. Since the road has come to an end, I will have to walk in. I get out of the truck and survey the area. The sun is shining. It is deathly quiet. I feel vulnerable and very ill at ease. I leave the truck door wide open, just in case. In case of what? I don't know, but I start walking.

There are no tracks in the snow; it is completely undisturbed. I can smell something like the sticky heaviness of fresh blood.

Sometimes, I get wafts of what smells like rotting flesh. My heart is pounding. My muscles feel stiff and tense. I remember too late that I should have brought the tire iron with me that I have kept behind the driver's seat as a readily available weapon should I ever need it.

I am almost to the cabin now. It is so very quiet, not a sound. A putrid stench catches in my throat. I can't breathe. There is evidence of recent footprints immediately around the cabin. And there, there in the snow, are drops of bright red blood.

Then, without warning, a shock surges through my body as I hear the sudden, metallic, uncoiling rip of a chain, only an arm's length away, followed by the gnashing, snarling, drooling, frothing, sucking, baring of teeth. It is a tan and smoky black-tipped German Shepherd. It rears up on its hind legs, straining at the collar and chain, barking and growling with a voraciousness I have never experienced before.

I run up and onto the veranda where I see a large, rough, thick plank table with vestiges of old blood and animal hair stuck to it. I try the door. "Thank God!" I verbally exhale as it opens and I slam it shut behind me. Once inside, I stand motionless as my eyes adjust to the dimness of the room after having been in the glaring brightness of the sun on the snow. After a minute or so, I slowly take in the sights around me, unable to comprehend the horror of it all. I feel like I will be sick.

The smell of blood is everywhere and the stench of decomposing flesh persists. The cabin is a one-room, open-space design. One corner appears to be the kitchen area where there is a huge butcher block with an assortment of knives hanging overhead. Bloody aprons and rags lie heaped in a corner. And hanging overhead, in what appears to be a sitting area by a large sunny window are pairs and pairs of sacs like little leather boxing gloves.

Suddenly, the door crashes open. A large, well-built man stands in the doorway. He is wearing a buckskin leather jacket, khaki pants, and mukluks. His mop of dark, dirty, curly hair is contained under a wool toque, knit in what appears to be a commercial combination of fleur-de-lis and an Indigenous Raven design. He has a hunting rifle in his hand, and he makes no effort to silence or halt the ferocious onslaught of the dog. He just stands there staring, not taking his eyes off me.

I am trapped. A sense of utter hopelessness and helplessness consumes me. If I try to run, the dog will surely break loose and attack me. If I do nothing, I will surely be butchered in this place of horror. I feel frozen in place, unable to move.

The man comes toward me. My hand instinctively goes up in defence. I try to speak but only manage a raspy whisper as I say "don't hurt me." I think I am going to faint.

Then I feel a wooden chair being shoved in behind my knees. "Think you better sit down," the man says.

I do as he says and feel the blood returning to my head. The man has moved away and is just standing staring at me. I fearfully and apologetically start to stutter and stammer "I just ran inside to get away from the dog. If you can just hang on to your dog, sir, I will leave, be on my way."

The man asks "What are you doing here in the first place? I saw a truck when I walked in. Is that yours? Are you alone?"

I feel certain that I don't appear to be an intimidating nor threatening intruder in any way. I am afraid to tell him that I alone. I just reply "Yes, that's my truck."

"I'm going to ask you one more time, what are you doing here in the first place?" the man adamantly persists.

"I'm looking for my brother," I reply, thinking to myself that surely one look at my little truck would suggest that I have purposefully driven through hell to get here. "I won't bother you further, I just want to locate my brother."

"Whose your brother, what's his name?" the man asks.

"Adam, Adam Charpentier," I reply. "I was told he lives around here. Do you know him?" I implore.

The man closely scrutinizes my face as he asks "Where are you from? How did you find this place?"

I feel afraid. I feel like I'm at a point of no return. My mind is racing as I once again deliberate my options for escape. I conclude that I best resort to just telling the man what he wants to know. I candidly tell him "My name is Julie Charpentier; I'm Adam's sister. I'm from Toronto. I flew to Edmonton and drove from there. Please—any information you have that might help me find my brother would be so helpful."

The man changes the subject and informs me "there's still some coffee left from this morning." "I'll get us some," he offers. He proceeds to pour us each an enamel cupful from a matching blue, speckled, enamel pot. He gestures for me to join him at a tiny table under the kitchen window.

The coffee is sour, strong, and full of grounds. The man doesn't seem to notice, and I don't really care as it distracts me from the stench and smell of blood all around and it eases the dryness in my throat.

The man continues to stare at me intently. My fears run rampant. What is he planning to do to me, I ask myself? I don't take my eyes off him either.

Still staring at me, but void of any expression, the man flatly states "I'm your brother."

I feel my eyes widen and my mouth open in utter disbelief. No, this can't be, I think to myself, I would surely recognize my own brother. I tell myself that my brother would never live like this.

The man shoves his chair back and goes outside, commanding the dog to be quiet!

He promptly returns and again seats himself at the kitchen table. His blank, sterile expression softens, and even seems, perhaps, con-ciliatory. He talks for a long time now, filling in the gaps from the time he had left home in Toronto.

Difficult as it is to comprehend, but based on everything the man has now told me, I feel assured that this is Adam, this is my brother. He is a lot older and a lot heavier than I remember him but, studying his face and mannerisms, and listening to his voice over these last minutes, I know it is him.

After a somewhat lengthy pause, his hands fumble with his coffee cup and he asks "How's our Dad doing?"

In desperation, yet at the same time with relief, I say "Adam, it's now over a year and a half since our dad died, and that is why I have been trying to find you."

Tears well up in Adam's eyes as he confesses "I do feel remorseful about the months having turned into years, about having made no contact at all with you and Dad. The way I have dealt with my perception of the problems at home has been, to say the least, needlessly harsh. I really have not contributed to any kind of a helpful nor gratifying resolution." His head and shoulders droop, and his hands rest flaccidly in his lap, as he shares with such a tiredness in his voice "It's just that I had felt so angry and bitter; I just wanted to lash out and leave."

"Over time," Adam continues, "I came to realize that our father had not been to blame for our mother leaving. I know now that the match between our parents was not a good one, and that making any attempt at a future together would have been futile. I believe, too, that our mother probably did love us, but had to leave us behind when she left because she had no income, no means with which to take care of us. I think she knew, deep in her heart, that our father was a good man, a good parent, and would do his very best to take good care of us."

I passionately endorse everything he has said and reply "Adam, you're not alone in the way that you had felt. I too, experienced such a deep emotional pain, and still do, knowing that our mother left us, and worse yet, as far as we know, has never even made any attempt to reconnect with us." We simultaneously reach out to hold each other's hand. A meditative silence prevails in the stillness. We gaze at each other with tears in our eyes and a newfound understanding. We mutually agree that it's time to just let her go—together. Adam clears his throat and momentarily stands to look out the window. Then he makes us a fresh pot of coffee and brings me some.

My inquiries turn to the strange objects and conditions around me. Adam seems eager to explain as he tells me "I eke out a living as a trapper and sustain myself by living off the land. I trade or sell the hides of the deer, moose, and elk that I shoot, along with the pelts of any coyote, beaver, or rabbits I have trapped." "With that income," he claims, "I can stock up on other staple supplies that I need; I buy those in Red Earth." He goes on to say "As a hunter, I also do my own butchering. I eat the red meat I get from the deer, elk, and moose. On occasion, I trap a beaver and will eat that too. In the summer months, I can go fishing. I especially savour the intense, fresh, flavour of wild berries, mushrooms, fiddleheads, and other greens that I can collect in the summertime."

"What are those little hanging pouches over there?" I motion to him, as I turn my head in their direction.

"Oh those," he says. "I'm drying beaver castors. They're the internal glands in a beaver that secrete a substance called castoreum. Both the male and female excrete it in order to mark their territory."

Adam is starting to relax now, and seems excited that I am showing an interest. "Let me show you how I make oil tinctures or paste from the beaver castors," he offers, getting up from his chair and moving toward a work table by the sitting area window. "I sell or trade those as bear or other wildlife bait lure when I take my hides and pelts in to Red Earth." He goes into great detail to both show and tell me about the whole process of making this paste and oil tincture. "Once the castors are dried, that is the best time to squeeze out the oil. Here, smell some," he encourages me.

Grudgingly, I comply. "Whoa!" I exclaim. "The castoreum oil, it smells a lot like vanilla, or maybe some kind of fruity smell." Adam is obviously pleased with my reaction.

He goes on to explain, "I next cut out the mid-sections of the fibrous connective tissue, slice the remaining castor, and using a glycerin emollient recipe, grind the castors into a paste in a food chopper. Then I puree the paste and remove any leftover membranous casing or fibrous tissue." "I get busy with other things tho'," he adds, "and if I can't get the whole process completed in a timely manner, I just store the dried castors in small, absorbent paper bags, and put them into the freezer-but only for a short period of time or they'll dry out."

I stay with Adam for ten days. We walk and talk through his daily routines. I eat whatever he cooks, go out on his trap lines with him, and accompany him hunting. Sometimes, we leave the dog to guard the place, and sometimes we take him along. His name is Ryker, and now that he knows that I belong, he is my devoted friend.

The ten days go by quickly, and we finally confront the reality that it is time for me to return to my way of life, and for Adam to remain in his. In the freshness of the open air, we embrace, and hold each other close. We have clearly kindled a strong brotherly-sisterly affection for each other. As we say our goodbyes, we vow that we will forever stay in touch. We will plan to see each other again and, if possible, often. It is emotionally too much right now to committedly know when that will be.

Ryker licks at my fingers and whines. We cry. Over these last days, Adam has disclosed "I've found an inner peace living in this remoteness." And he has calmly and confidently told me "I will die here, living off the grid."

Adam helps carry my things as we make our way to my truck. Ryker sits facing my door, his head cocked slightly to one side, intermittently crying as I get into the driver's side, adjust my seat, and get comfortable while the motor warms. I extend my left arm to Adam and we hug cheek to cheek one last time. I tell him "I love you bro'." Adam remains silent but hugs me harder. "'Bye Ryker," I add, as I wave and, reluctantly, close my door.

I slowly roll away from the meadow clearing and my brother's log cabin, toward the quiet dark of the forest, waving back as long as I can see them in my rear view mirror. All the while, tears stream down my face. I do believe we have both felt a satisfying calm and resolve in having reconnected. But I could never live this lifestyle, and he, on the other hand, has found an inner peace living alone in isolation. My heart is both happy and hurting.

I sadly contemplate the long road home. I have no timeline and decide that is for the best considering my arduous journey in getting here. I determine to just take it one day at a time. I have decided to return on the same route as I had come, in part, due to a familiarity now, Adam's advice that the highway that goes directly to Slave Lake will be in no better condition, and to hopefully locate and make contact with a friend of Adam's at East Prairie Metis Settlement. Having reached the intersection, I turn south on Highway AB-67 (relabelled to AB-88 in 1988) toward Red Earth Creek.

Immediately upon my arrival, I check in at the same mobile trailer motel where I had previously stayed. I had told Adam that I would be staying here for a couple of days in order to pick up a few supplies and to get my truck serviced and checked over thoroughly. I find it helps to alleviate the heavy sadness that I feel, to have to be thinking forward now, to have to focus on a specific plan for the trip ahead.

It is now the third day after having left Adam's place, and every-thing has gone as planned. I am departing Red Earth Creek early this morning, but already I find the muskeg is softer than when I had come due to the spring thaw, and I need to pay close attention to staying on the packed road surface.

Just before turning off Highway AB-67 (relabelled AB-88 in 1988) on to Highway AB-750 to drive in a southwesterly direction toward the Atikameg Indigenous Community, I can see ahead, on my side of the road, a small black truck that has slid sideways off the road surface at a downward angle. As I approach it more closely, I see that the rear bumper and wheels are deeply embedded in mud, and it is clearly obvious that the driver had been spinning the back wheels for some time in an attempt to get out of this boggy mess. I also notice a thick and stubby radio antenna coming from the mid-rear of the cab roof and deduce that, in all likelihood, this is a government or corporate fleet vehicle, and therefore, probably not the driver's first trip on these roads. The road is busy and narrow. My grip tightens on my steering wheel and I check my mirrors with utmost care before pulling out to go around the vehicle. I do not want to obstruct nor hold up any passing or oncoming traffic. I tell myself to remember this incident as a fair warning toward being extra cautious with regard to the road conditions from here on.

Adam had advised me that I could expect the Loon Lake Indigenous Settlement, the Atikameg Indigenous Community, and the Gift Lake Metis Settlement to all be quiet as most of the people are usually out hunting or on their trap lines. "Even the children," he had said, "may not have been in school for days." "Some would call it truancy," he had explained, "but it's really not. It's their way of life here, a way of learning from and bonding with the elders, and a way of being in harmony with the nature around them." "It's a good life, really," he had gone on "when there's plentiful moose and fish to cook up fresh, salt, dry, or smoke."

"On the other hand," he had continued with a grin, "one of the down sides of living out here in the bush, as I think you can already attest to, is the absence of some of the luxuries in life, like running water and being able to take a bath for example. The black flies are thick out here in the summertime and those noseeums are tenacious. Both leave stinging bites that prompt one to itch and scratch like crazy. In turn, that causes a lot of inflammation, and even infection and oozing sores if a person can't soothe and cleanse the areas properly. There's nothing like good ol' soap and water for that, and personally, I dab on a little baking soda paste, as well, if I can. The kids are especially plagued because they don't stop and think like an adult might—just keep scratching with dirty hands, making it worse."

My recollections from my time spent with Adam help the time go more quickly as I pass through the Atikameg Indigenous Community and the Gift Lake Metis Settlement. I feel so alone and vulnerable and wonder what I will do in future when it comes time for Adam and I to visit again. I don't think I will ever be able to convince him to come to the big city for a meetup and he would have to leave Ryker behind to guard his place-not exactly a socialized animal to be bringing to the city. I think the worst part of the drive is behind me now, and I pull over on a trucker rest stop by a scenic marshy swamp in order to get out and stretch my legs and relax for a bit.

The air is damp and pure; I breathe it in deeply, and breathe again. I can see beaver, busily carrying gnawed off aspen tree trunks, swimming toward their dam sites where they will strategically place them. I hear the sound of a forlorn loon. Geese fly northward over-head, in a V-formation. I return to my truck and sit sideways on the passenger side with the door open in order to absorb the peaceful view in front of me. I break open a refreshing drink and some snacks that I had picked up while in Red Earth Creek. I soon feel somewhat rejuvenated and decide I had better get back on the road.

I mindlessly drive for some time when, suddenly, I come to my senses. I realize I have not been as focused on the landscape around me as I should have been and I have missed a crucial bend in the road. Inadvertently, that error has led me straight ahead and on to a different cut line which is not a road at all. I am lost.

The evening darkness is now settling into the trees. I cannot and do not want to turn around. I know I am still driving in a southerly direction as the sun is setting to my right. It is a rough ride, and I hope I will not get hung up on a tree stump. If I can keep going, I feel certain I will come out to a crossroad at some point. I continue to drive through the cut line clearing, constantly peering ahead, looking for any stumps.

Finally-there it is: Highway AB-2. "What a relief!" I shout as I make my way on to an approach and turn west to head back to the town of High Prairie. I immediately check in at the Borealis Motor Inn and Grill, assured of finding much needed accommodations for the night and a hot meal. I wonder if Lena will be at work in the restaurant tonight. I have so much to tell her.

Checked-in and calmed down, I go for dinner. Lena is not here as I had hoped. Feeling restored with a full stomach, I return to my room. It is warm, clean, and comfortable and I feel safe. I prepare for bed and an early start in the morning.

I sleep well but I am emotionally exhausted and struggle with a pervasive sadness. I am missing Adam, and I feel so alone. Lena is not in the restaurant again this morning as I force down a fast but hearty breakfast and coffee. Perhaps that is just as well, I tell myself, as I really don't have time to be visiting. However, I ask the owner to let her know that I had passed through and that I had asked about her.

Once packed up and outside, I proceed to gas up, check my oil, top my washer fluid, clean my windows, and check my tires. As planned, I am out on Highway AB-2 early and heading east toward Slave Lake.

But first, there is the stop along the way that I need to think about. Adam and I had talked a great deal about his life, from the time he had left Toronto to his finally having settled in Peace country. His journey northward had not been uneventful either. He told me about one incident that, to this day, stood out in his memory:

"It had been a stormy night and I was just east of High Prairie by the East Prairie Metis Settlement turnoff when my vehicle broke down. I became stranded, freezing in the cold for several hours and was getting desperate, hoping someone would come by. Then I heard the high-pitched whine of a nearby skidoo, and I could see a bouncing beam penetrating through the whiteout conditions. My battery wasn't quite dead, and I frantically starting flashing my headlights On and Off, On and Off, On and Off. Please, please, let the driver see me, I remember thinking. I didn't dare leave my truck, the drifts were so deep, and the storm so blinding. Thankfully, when I saw the beam turn toward me, I knew the skidoo driver had seen me, and it wasn't long before he was slipping up along side of me.

I remember him yelling 'Somebody in there need help?'

I had trouble rolling my window down but when I finally managed it, I yelled back that I'd never been so happy to see anyone in my life. I told him that my truck had broken down and that I'd been out here for hours.

He readily confirmed my sentiments and yelled back 'It's a bad one alright.' He told me he'd already had to go rescue one of his neighbours and take him home and that's why he was out on a night like this. He firmly agreed 'You're going to freeze to death out here for sure,' and then, without any hesitation at all, he told me 'Better get on, in back of me, and I'll take you back to my place. It's not far. Get you warmed up and something to eat.'

I spent the night there, in his trailer out in East Prairie. Around noon, after the storm had subsided, he had a landline and called around to get me some help to tow my truck into High Prairie to a garage so I could get it fixed. The guy saved my life. I'll never forget that. I told him if I ever came back that way I would look him up, that I was so thankful. It's been years now since that happened, and it haunts me that I never got back there to see him again. I never go past Red Earth, don't need to. You know that. But I've never forgotten what he did for me.

Julie, I'm concerned about your travelling out here alone, don't know how things will go for you. But if you are doing okay, if you have the time, I wonder if you would possibly consider going out to this guy's place—just to say hello from me, and let him know where

I ended up in case he's ever up this way. His name is Huritt Richard and I'll give you the directions; it's not far off the highway. I have no right to ask you, I know, but it would mean so much to me."

"Adam," I mutter out loud, "I am going to make the time." I know I would never be able to live with myself, forgive myself, knowing I had been right here at the East Prairie Metis Settlement turnoff, and had then driven right by, never even having tried to locate his friend. I know how special it would be for them to make contact again. However, if I do find him, I will have to explain that I have to keep the visit short, as I'm trying to make Edmonton at a reasonable hour tonight.

According to Adam's directions, I should be only minutes away. As I turn south off the highway into the East Prairie Metis Settlement, much to my amazement, there-immediately on my left, is a majestic moose with a large, dangling bell and a massive rack. He is standing absolutely motionless, just staring at me. I stop on the side of the road to take a closer look at this awesome creature. I decide he is a musing moose, and name him Magnus. What a delightful start to my day!

The winding road into the settlement is so very quiet, as if driving on carpet. The tires creep over the fresh new blanket of soft snow, and furry hoar frost clings to the wild grasses and weeds. The sun comes out as I round a bend, the rays bursting through the spruce and sparkling like millions of encrusted diamonds on the snow.

I twist and turn southward along a winding road that takes me further into the settlement. Then, across an open sun-filled meadow, I see a trailer, nestled below a canopy of overhanging boughs. That should be his place, I think to myself.

As I leave the road to drive along his lane way, I notice that he is working around his trailer, shaking the snow from the boughs and shovelling a clear path to his vehicle. He seems to hear me approaching and stands erect, looking toward me. Oh my, I think to myself, what a proud and noble presence his tallness conveys.

"Good Morning, Sir," I call out, as I exit my truck and start toward him with a friendly smile. His facial expression is serious and he listens intently while I quickly explain "I'm looking for a man by the name of Huritt Richard. My brother gave me directions to here and I think I should be at the right place. His name is Adam Charpentier. Do you remember him? You helped him out a few years ago during a storm, but he has never forgotten your kindness and, actually, still feels indebted to you, that you saved his life. I have been up north to visit him, and he had asked, if at all possible, could I try and make contact with Huritt for him, bring him up to date with regard to his whereabouts."

The man's demeanor completely relaxes, his mouth opens in dismay, and tears well up in his eyes. He puts down the shovel, removes his mitts, and steps forward to extend his open hand. I accept his gesture, placing my hand in his. I feel such an unexpected and deep connection as he gently folds my hand into his with his other, and momentarily and warmly holds it.

"I am so pleased to meet you, and yes, I am Huritt and you are at the right place," he informs me, while happily smiling. "Please-come in. I will make us some tea and we can chat."

"Oh, that would be wonderful," I reply.

Huritt offers me his arm as we ascend the steps on his deck around the trailer, and he advises me, "Careful, these can get pretty slippery with a light dusting of snow on them."

He guides me into an adjoining sun room where he offers me a comfortable chair. He disappears into his kitchen and soon returns to set fine china before me on a white cloth. He goes back to the kitchen and next emerges with a steaming, aromatic pot of tea. "I prepare this from a blend of dried and crushed tea leaves that I hand-pick in the forest," he proudly tells me.

We make small chatter at first as we discuss the day and we drink our tea. I find myself absolutely mesmerized by Huritt's dignified eloquence. Cognizant of my time constraints, however, I soon emphasize my travel plan to get to Edmonton before it gets too late tonight. Huritt is most understanding and does not interrupt as I quickly share what I know of Adam's coming to have settled north of Red Earth Creek, and how to get there. We finish our tea, and I tell Huritt "I really should be going. I am so thankful to have made your acquaintance and I will mail Adam to let him know all about our visit when I get back to Toronto. I cannot tell you how happy he will be."

Huritt seems so very emotionally moved by this visit. He interjects to say "I wish you could stay longer as this has been so very special to me. I promise I won't keep you but, I would like to invite you to walk with me-for just a bit."

We quickly put on our coats, and venture out into the sunshine. As we begin to walk, a feeling of peace envelops me. He teaches me and reads to me from the trees. Mother Earth and creatures speak to him. And he listens and he hears. He knows when it will be a long, cold winter. He knows when spring will come early. He is patient, gentle, and wise. "It is time for you to go now, Julie," he reminds me. "I will always treasure this time we have had together," and he reluctantly escorts me back to my truck.

"Thank you, Huritt, thank you for everything," I genuinely express, as I wave to him and back out of the lane way. The interior of the truck has become so warm in the sunshine, and feels like a warm embrace around me.

I wind my way back to the highway and continue east. I find this stretch of the trip rather boring-no trees, nothing to look at but open space and stubby, dry, prairie grass. However, I have been able to reflect on the pleasant visit with Huritt and that has certainly helped to occupy my mind.

I am soon passing by the community of Driftpile and the landscape slowly starts to change. The forest, although sparce, is beginning to reappear, and I find that heartening as it means I am getting close to the town of Slave Lake. As the miles go by, the forest becomes more dense.

I am also keenly aware of the increasing frequency of logging trucks on the highway, transporting full loads of logs toward Edmonton. It's frustrating and a little frightening to be stuck in behind one of these extended loads. Not only is there is the irritating flap of the red warning flags secured to the ends of these loads, but I also envision what would happen to me and my little truck should those chains that secure the logs to the flatbed trailer, ever snap. The oncoming traffic is steady. I'm also driving into the sun and it's sometimes difficult to see up ahead when I attempt to pull out to pass. The heat of the day has created a low fog in the area, too, and I put my headlights On.

I am so close to Slave Lake now but I just can't seem to make time on this busy road. I keep veering to my left in order to peer up ahead, waiting for an opportunity to pass. I wait for what seems an eternity and, at last, I make a break for it, depressing the gas pedal to the floor in order to get by this long load as quickly as possible. I am steadily gaining and neck and neck with the cab of the truck beside me. Suddenly! . . . the blast of a horn. I can barely make out something looming toward me in the fog . . .

. . .

. . . There are so many voices. I can't move. I can't see. I think I'm on a bed, in a room. I am so cold. The pain is so bad. Why are there things in my mouth, and things stuck into my arms? I can hear things beeping. I must be in a hospital. I feel like I am fading in and out. I don't know what is happening . . .

. . .

. . . A male voice is demanding "She can't wait. She won't make it. We need to move her now. Start working on it." I feel like there's people all around me. I keep fading away . . .

. . .

. . . A female voice is asking "Julie, can you hear me? Tell us the name of your next of kin."

"Adam," I quickly answer. I want the voice to hear me. I hope the voice can hear me.

"Adam what? Julie. What is Adam's last name? Is it Charpentier like you?" the female voice persists.

"Yes," I manage to reply.

"Good, Julie—Adam Charpentier," the female voice is saying. "Where does he live, Julie? Where does Adam live?" the female voice is wanting to know.

I can't think. I can't remember. But then I do remember and I say "Red."

"Red Earth, Julie. Does Adam live at Red Earth Creek?" the female voice continues to press.

"Yes," I reply.

A male voice is confirming "Okay, we're on it, we'll find him." I keep fading away . . .

. . .

. . . A male voice is agitatedly explaining "It's a two seater, single-engine, light aircraft. The fog's getting worse. I'll be flying by sight alone. We need to get going if we're going to make Edmonton. There's a limit load factor as well. I need Julie's approximate weight and you need to send the lightest smallest nurse you got." I don't understand what is happening. I keep fading away . . .

. . .

. . . "Julie, can you hear me?" a soft voice is asking.

Why is there such a roaring noise around me, I wonder.

"Julie, I am holding your hand," a soft voice is saying. "Squeeze if you can hear me."

I think I am squeezing but I can't tell.

"Good job, Julie," the voice is confirming. I keep fading away . . .

. . .

. . . "We're in the air, Julie. I am your nurse," the soft voice is saying.

Suddenly, it feels like we are falling, everything is shaking, then . . . Hit! with a bang.

"You okay back there?" a man is shouting. "It's going to be a pretty rough ride. The turbulence is real bad."

The soft voice is saying, "We're here," and I can feel her body banging against me.

. . . I keep fading away . . . Sometimes I can feel that my feet are so hot, but my body is so cold. I think there's heat blasting from somewhere . . . I keep fading away . . . There is so much noise. Sometimes, I think I hear the man yelling and the soft voice answering . . . I keep fading away . . .

. . .

. . . "Make it fast, she's going to the OR right away, what can you tell me?" a male voice is demanding . . . I keep fading away . . .

. . .

. . . "Your surgery is finished, Julie" a female voice is saying. "Adam is coming, he's on his way. Hang in there, Julie, Adam is coming."

"Adam-Adam. I saw your friend," I whisper.

The female voice is saying that she is listening.

"Adam, don't leave me." . . . I keep fading away . . .

The meadow is warm . . . in the sunshine all year 'round. And I am wrapped with a blanket that Huritt gave Adam for me; it has an Indigenous arrow design on it. Ryker presides over me when he is at home and not out on the trap lines or hunting. Adam visits with me every day, sometimes quietly laughing, sometimes reminiscing, sometimes telling jokes, and sometimes shedding tears. And in the summertime, he brings me wild flowers. I am at peace. It is a natural place—a place where Adam and I will forever be together.

CPSIA information can be obtained
at www.ICGtesting.com
Printed in the USA
BVHW080148090622
639024BV00002B/10